DAINTY, SHY, AND RETIRING?
NOT ON YOUR LIFE!

Olive Oatman — futilely struggling to shield her mother from being bludgeoned to death, then marching as a captive through the desert, barefoot and without water for days.

Ida Genung — her new baby by her side, fighting to save a bleeding neighbor in his lonely cabin, hours from any help.

Larcena Pennington — crawling down a snowy mountain for weeks to reach help after Apaches had stabbed her, thrown her off a ledge, stoned her with boulders, and left her for dead.

GREEN AND UNTRIED OR
ROUGH AND READY, THESE

STALWART WOMEN

stubbornly stood steady against any onslaught
and refused to back down or give in.
Yes, they personified culture and home life
in god-forsaken outbacks, but they
could be tough without comment or ego.
They baked pies for visitors and shot intruders,
planted gardens and dug out bullets,
devotedly cared for the abandoned
and vengefully pursued killers
— never expecting any prize but survival.

෴ ෴ ෴ ෴ ෴

Read other books in the
WILD WEST COLLECTION,
fast-paced, real-life stories of when the Old West
was still young and rowdy, where anything
could happen — and too often did.

෴ ෴ ෴ ෴ ෴

DAYS OF DESTINY
MANHUNTS & MASSACRES
THEY LEFT THEIR MARK
THE LAW OF THE GUN
TOMBSTONE CHRONICLES

Turn to the back of this book to read more about them.

Design: MARY WINKELMAN VELGOS
Copy Editor: CHARLES BURKHART AND EVELYN HOWELL
Research: JEB STUART ROSEBROOK
Production: ELLEN STRAINE
Photographic enhancement: VICKY SNOW
Front cover art: VERYL GOODNIGHT
Tooled leather design on covers: KEVIN KIBSEY AND RONDA JOHNSON-FREEMAN

Prepared by the Book Division of *Arizona Highways*® magazine, a monthly
publication of the Arizona Department of Transportation.

Publisher — Nina M. La France
Managing Editor — Bob Albano
Associate Editor — Evelyn Howell
Art Director — Mary Winkelman Velgos
Production Director — Cindy Mackey

Printed in the United States
Library of Congress Catalog Number 99-61929
ISBN 0-916179-77-X

STALWART WOMEN

by LEO BANKS

Book Editor:
BOB ALBANO

Leo W. Banks grew up in Boston. As a schoolboy, he delved into history as a hobby, "publishing" books based on his reading and other research, mostly of the Civil War.

He would read articles about the war and its generals, then write his version of the stories, hand-binding the typed pages. He even got his father, a math professor, to write glowing introductions for the "books."

He graduated from Boston College in 1975 with a degree, not surprisingly, in history and moved to Arizona the next year. In 1977, he earned a master's degree in journalism from the University of Arizona in Tucson.

For the past 20 years, Leo has traveled Arizona extensively, searching out obscure historical details in libraries and archives. He has focused on the Territorial years and the Apache wars. Over the last decade, Leo has written numerous articles for *Arizona Highways* magazine, not just history pieces, but travel and adventure stories as well.

Many of Leo's pieces appear in books published by *Arizona Highways*. He wrote the historical accounts in *Grand Canyon Stories: Then and Now* (to be published in September, 1999), and most of the stories in *Days of Destiny* and *Manhunts & Massacres*, also in the Wild West Collection. And Leo is one of the authors of *Travel Arizona II*, a guidebook.

He has worked as a reporter for the *Arizona Daily Star* in Tucson, as a correspondent for the *Los Angeles Times* and *Boston Globe*, and has written numerous articles for *Sports Illustrated*, *National Geographic Traveler*, and other magazines.

Leo lives in Tucson with his wife, Teresa, and son, Patrick.

Veryl Goodnight, whose sculpture *No Turning Back* is on the cover of *Stalwart Women*, has placed work in private and corporate collections throughout the United States, Europe, and Japan for a quarter century. Her monuments are on public display at the Cowboy Hall of Fame in Oklahoma City, the Houston Astrodome, the Pro-Rodeo Hall of  Fame, Brookgreen Gardens in South Carolina, the Lely Resort in Naples, Florida, and other locations, including several universities and the Denver Zoo.

Her seven-ton monument to freedom, *The Day the Wall Came Down*, is an edition of only two "sister" castings — one for the United States and one for Germany. The U.S. casting is permanently on display at the Bush Presidential Library at Texas A&M University, and the U.S. Air Force flew the "sister" casting to Berlin's historic Tempelhof airport on June 26, 1998, the 50th anniversary of the start of the Berlin Airlift.

In February, 1995, *Art of the West* ran a major article featuring her Western women and poetry, *The Goodnight Girls*, with her sculpture *Passing Times* on the cover (the first time in 10 years that *Art of the West* chose a sculpture for its cover).

Veryl's sculptures are on display at Trailside Americana Galleries in Scottsdale, Arizona, and Jackson Hole, Wyoming, and at Altermann & Morris Galleries, Santa Fe, New Mexico, and Dallas, Texas. She also participates in prestigious exhibits including Artists of America in Denver, Colorado, and the Governor's Invitational in Cheyenne, Wyoming.

Veryl and her husband, Roger Brooks, live just north of Santa Fe with a menagerie of animals. Roger, a retired commercial airline pilot, manages the studio business and still flies for fun. Their favorite pastime is riding their horses.

Besides sculpting *No Turning Back*, she expressed the concept in a poem, which appears on Page 144.

CONTENTS

The Price and the Prize:
Hardship and Sacrifice
for Survival
and a Place in History

"I never saw a white woman for nine whole months, and I have taken my drinking water from holes in the ground and been glad to get it."
— Elizabeth Heiser, rancher

WE MAY CLAIM TO KNOW THE MEANING OF WORDS SUCH AS hardship, sacrifice, and endurance, but it's a phantom knowledge. For the real thing, we can turn to the experiences of Arizona's pioneer women. Their stories — infrequently told — are in memoirs, diaries, letters, newspapers, and oral transcripts in libraries and historical societies.

The modern reader may gasp at what the American frontier demanded of women. Most striking is how the survivors (an appropriate term) tell of their life experiences in words that for the most part are unadorned. Nineteenth-century women had a capacity to see their lives clearly and to express their joys and travails without self-analysis and rumination.

She didn't think too much about her situation; she didn't have time. From the call of the cock to the yip of the coyote, there was work to be done.

And if she did have the time, how would thinking change the situation? Thinking about it wouldn't make it easier to sleep on the ground in Apache country, wouldn't draw a rifle bead on a deer that had to fall if her children were to eat.

Stress comes in different packages for different times, and pain seems to be relative, depending on the century.

**ARIZONA TERRITORY RANCHER ELIZABETH HEISER
IN A RUSTIC POSE, CIRCA 1894.**

Consider Coralie Mix Converse, an Army wife at Camp Lincoln in central Arizona, not far from the present site of Fort Verde. One morning in 1867, this lively 19-year-old cinched herself into her corseted riding habit and rode 56 miles to Prescott, sidesaddle. She stabled her horse, took a bath, changed into her evening gown, and still had enough spark to dance all night at the governor's ball. To put the feat into perspective: A normal day's march for cavalry was 40 miles.

Fifty days after her epic ride, Coralie's husband was badly wounded in action and became an invalid. For the next 34 years, she tended to him on a disability pension of $62 a month.

Coralie was a woman of sand, as the saying went in those days, although it was applied only to men. Truth was, the Arizona Territory had lots of sand, not many women. The 1860 census for what now is Arizona showed a total population of 6,482, including about 20 women for every 100 men. Most of the women were Mexicans; there were 44 Anglo women. Ten years later, the population approached 10,000, and the ratio increased to 42 women for every 100 men.

According to historian Bob Munson, manager of Fort Verde State Historic Park, the national population was 30 million in 1865, when the Civil War ended, but in the first decade after the war, only a million people came to the West.

"That's 3 percent of the population, and the bulk of that is men," says Munson. "With the exception of a few, unmarried men, the concept of the adventurous pioneer is false. Most of those who came West had to come because they had washed out in the East."

The women who did come were almost always following their men. If a woman came unattached — a rarity, and a bit of a scandal in those still-Victorian times — she didn't stay that way for long, not with the lopsided number of lonesome men.

In August, 1869, a wagon train full of emigrants pulled into sizzling Gila Bend. Among the passengers was a young woman named Mary Taylor, traveling mate of a Mr. Nash, referred to among the party as her husband, although they had not yet married. By the time they reached Arizona, the thought of a life with Nash gave Mary heartburn.

"I was tired of the trip, and my husband and I had been fussing," she told a friend later. "So I said, 'Where I can, I'll leave this outfit.' A big man sitting on his horse at the campfire heard me say it. He said, 'Lady, if you want to leave these people . . . I'll take you. I live a few miles west and will protect you.' I was so desperate, so I told him I would go with him. He said, 'Get on behind me and hold onto my belt.' "

The man told Mary he already had a housekeeper, a Mexican woman, but Mary would be the lady of the house. Next morning they embarked on a two-day ride to Yuma to buy clothes for Mary. "As we rode home he talked of his experiences like reading a novel. Next day we had a heart-to-heart talk. And I became Mrs. Woolsey."

The courtship of King Woolsey, one of Arizona's storied Indian fighters, and Mary Taylor Woolsey, who became a prominent land owner and a wealthy businesswoman, wasn't particularly unusual. Alone, Mary had no place to go and

STANWIX STATION WAS KING WOOLSEY'S HOME AND ARIZONA TERRITORY'S SECOND TELEGRAPH STATION.

faced many dangers. King had few white women to woo. Dire circumstance often percolated the chemistry of love.

Sarah Butler York came West in 1873 from central Missouri in a party of 16 wagons. On the Great Plains, their greatest problem was a lack of firewood.

"It was some time before the women would consent to use a fire made of buffalo chips," said Sarah, in the *Arizona Historical Review* for July, 1928. "Afterwards we made a joke of it, and would laugh to see some of the fastidious young men come into camp with a sack of chips on their shoulders. The old chips that had laid for years through all kinds of weather certainly made a wonderful fire."

Sarah praised the Mexican drovers who worked through cold and snow to keep the wagons moving.

"They were good to the children and would want to hold them," she wrote. "This would have been a rest for me, as I had to hold my baby all day to keep her from falling out of the wagon. But they were so filthy and infested with vermin I didn't dare allow them to help me."

Life didn't get much easier on arrival.

The houses of pioneers were usually adobes and had mud floors, at least until lumber could be cut and a board floor installed. To make her ranch house more homey, Dora

Hammels Fowler papered the walls with newspapers, the only material available. But the sandstorms that blew up at her ranch, 14 miles west of Phoenix, tore through the cracks in the walls and shredded the paper, and the dust inside Dora's house became so thick she couldn't see.

If a woman happened to live in a well-appointed home, it became a social center. In a memoir compiled by author Oren Arnold, Mary Adaline Gray, the first white woman to settle in the Salt River Valley, remembered having as many as 50 people in her home.

"We'd doctor each other's sick, bury our dead," she said. "I bet a hundred funerals were preached in our place. We'd bring lovers together and have big parties to help 'em marry. Governors and congressmen and little pigheaded politicians would come and make their plans, a settin' at our big table. Cowboys and miners, trappers and soldiers would come visit."

Credit Gray's pretty decorations for a part of the attraction her house held for so many.

"They liked to set in chairs for hours on end, just looking at the inside of my house," she said. "They'd get up and finger my window curtains. I'd see 'em touch a lace doily like it would break. They'd stand in front of a vase of flowers or a pretty picture and just gawk at it."

In many homes, windows were nothing but rifle slits, handy in the event of Indian attack but not terribly stylish. Before leaving his ranch for extended periods, Sarah Butler York's husband would fill gunny sacks with sand and pack them halfway up the windows. Like every ranch wife, Sarah, who settled south of Clifton, spent hours barricaded inside her home, feeling the tingle of fear as she awaited the return of her husband and his cowhands.

"If the men were late in coming from their rides after the cattle, I was very uneasy and could not rest," she said.

"My husband would scoldingly say that he always trailed a cow until he found her, and that I must get used to his being away. I often told him the day might come when he would wish I would become uneasy and send men to hunt him. This proved true."

In the spring of 1881, George York was ambushed and killed by Indians while trying to retrieve stolen horses, and Sarah's bitterness never waned.

In her article, she called Apaches "great cowards who never fight in the open. A rattlesnake is a more honest enemy, because he, at least, warns one before striking."

The instinct to protect home and family often turned otherwise gentle women into tigresses. Jane Fourr was alone at her ranch near Tombstone when Indians rode up and demanded food. When she refused, an Indian knocked down her laundry line, sending wet clothes into the dirt. More angry than afraid, Jane whacked the Indian with a pole, smacked his horse on the rump, and sent the intruders galloping away.

On another occasion, according to the autumn 1945 issue of *Arizona Quarterly* magazine, a Mexican outlaw tried to force his way into Jane's home. She fired both barrels of her shotgun, blowing off his arm.

In 1874, Mrs. Fannie Stevens was with her three small children at Lonesome Ranch when Apaches struck. For hours she fought them off, shooting from the windows.

Late that day, cowboys heard the noise and drove the Indians away. "I'll take word to Mr. Stevens at town, ma'am," one cowboy volunteered. "Just write out whatever you want to say."

Mrs. Stevens deliberated, then wrote this message: "Dear Lewis, The Apaches came. I am mighty nigh out of buckshot. Please send me more. Your loving wife."

Necessity also turned the frontier into a kind of giant medical school for the pioneer woman. Canadian-born Elizabeth Aughey came to Fort Verde in 1872 as a laundress for the 5th Cavalry. She became the post's hospital matron and for 13 years supervised its staff and assisted the surgeon.

When the fort was abandoned in 1891, she stayed in the Verde Valley and became the family doctor to a generation of settlers. Married as a teenager to Joseph Young, Elizabeth Aughey Young aided in the delivery of numerous babies, until shortly before her death in 1905. By then known as Grandma Young, she was one of "nature's noble women," her obituary said, cranky, opinionated, and revered. It also said:

"None but the frontiersman and the prospector, that class who blaze the pathway and plant the family tree of civilization that others may follow, especially in Indian country . . . can truly appreciate the value of such a person."

The remedies used by such "doctors" often were handed down through families. Sometimes they were suggested by neighbors or friendly Indians familiar with herbal treatments. Much of it was folklore, but much of it worked.

Sadie Martin, who came with her family to the Gila Valley in 1888, cured her husband's dysentery by giving him this nightly dose: two cubes of crushed sugar mixed with the yolk of an egg. To treat her own rheumatism, she took dry cow manure, powdered it, and heated it. She put her arm in the powder and wrapped a cloth around it all to keep in the heat.

"John would get up about three or four times in the night to reheat the mixture," Sadie wrote in her recollections at the Arizona Historical Society. "Mother made more of a fuss about it than I did, as the odor was most unpleasant. . . . It was a heroic remedy but it brought results, and we could not be too particular about methods in the desert."

Such remedies couldn't replace the skills of a doctor, but a doctor was not always available because there were so few in the territory, distances were great, and communication was achingly slow. Sadie Martin's son, Brayton, fell ill so quickly that by the time she and John sent for help, it was too late.

"The Yuma doctor could only attend to sending a little gray casket," she wrote. "We had a few wild flowers and father read the burial service. It seemed that our one bright star had set. When I look back on that time, and think what the loss was to John and me, I can hardly see how we could have gone on, had we not meant so much to each other. We were so young and there was so little in that country for us."

If losing a child is life's supreme pain, grinding isolation

**ELIZABETH AUGHEY YOUNG
STANDING ON THE HOSPITAL PORCH AT FORT VERDE.**

might be second. Frances Cummins De Spain was 25 years old in 1873, when she, her husband, and her father landed in the small silver camp of Cedar, Arizona, making her the only female for miles. For eight months, Frances cooked meals on a camp fire, never once seeing another woman. To make matters more interesting, it rained almost continuously for six weeks.

Under such circumstances, to even see hope on the horizon must have required grit. Ranch women knew isolation.

"Several times I took a gun and went to the barking dogs and shot varmints by myself in the night when the men would be gone," said Nancy Price Conger, who lived in such remote locales that the sight of anything with a pulse was cause to break out the fiddle and dance. "I never heard but two or three sermons preached until I was grown."

Sadie Martin described a loneliness so intense that even dogs, horses, and chickens seemed to take on personalities. Encountering a "human being of any description assumed the proportions of an adventure."

Such thoughts provide insight into frontier hospitality. Look at it this way: If you hadn't seen another person in months, and a bedraggled stranger showed up at your door, mud caked to his face, something worse caked to his boots, the stench of a sun-baked stockyard hovering over the lice two-stepping through his hair, you would invite him in for a tin of black coffee and tackle him when he tried to leave.

With people, as with everything on the frontier, the pioneer woman made do with what she had.

A baby's bassinet might be a canned goods box, a pillow stuffed inside as a mattress. Young girls carded wool and spun yarn to make the family's clothes. Shoes often were made like an Indian's buckskin moccasins, the leather tanned by the men. Girls gathered wheat and rye straw from to braid into hats.

"We knitted our hose and mittens, crocheted our undershirts, hoods, and jackets," said Ellen Bates Newman, born in Winslow in 1877. "We helped grind wheat on a hand mill for our bread. Later a larger mill took its place; this was run by horse power."

Even caring for the dead was done at home. Lottie Tevis Edwards said that her mother, who lived at Bowie Station, always kept black sateen or calico on hand, a few yards of black lace and ribbon, and enough additional material to make a shroud.

"There were no undertakers or embalmers in those days closer than one hundred miles," said Lottie. "I have even seen my mother removing her last pair of white hose in order to pass them on for someone to be buried in."

When alone, the pioneer woman's role was wide open — whatever needed to be done. But when a man was around, her role was more strictly defined, although still huge: She was responsible for nurturing a civilization — through churches, clubs, libraries, families, homes, and schools.

In town after town in Arizona Territory, the first schools were started through the initiative of women, who, like Mary Adaline Gray, demanded learning for their young. At a public meeting in Phoenix in 1870, she rose and declared, "First public house you men build has got to be a school. We don't want our children to be brought up like little hellions. Get a teacher with some sense and pay him a fair wage."

The mother of Jennie Parks Ringgold, of Duncan, was known as a friend of the cowboys in sickness and trouble. Many of them came to town to dance in the old saloon building. At one dance, Jennie casually mentioned that the mothers of town were anxious for their kids to attend school. She suggested that the cowboys raise money to build one, which also could be used for their dances.

A collection was taken and up went the wood frame building, the only schoolhouse in Duncan until the late 1890s. Traveling ministers preached there.

"Often, if the crowd were large enough," Ringgold wrote, "the desks would be moved against the wall after services, and the floor would be cleared. Someone would go for Frank Taylor, the fiddler, and the dance would begin."

Jane Fourr's biggest problem in getting her children educated was her husband, William. He'd managed to get along without schooling and believed his kids could do the same. But Jane, who acceded to her man's wishes in everything else (even calling him Mr. Fourr), put her foot down on this one.

Every summer, she and the older children worked hard on the ranch, according to *Arizona Quarterly*. "In the fall — no matter what Mr. Fourr said — they loaded a few necessities onto wagons and drove to Tombstone, where Jane rented some empty house in which they half-lived, half-camped during the school year," the magazine reported. "The Fourr kids and their mom came to town in this way for 15 years."

The pioneer woman nourished the finer parts of life. She started social, religious, historical, garden, and reading clubs, such as the Shakespeare Reading Circle of Flagstaff, begun in 1892. It sounds quaint to us now, but culture served as a comforting barrier against the wildness all around.

At military posts, officers' wives organized picnics, dances, dinner and card parties, and theatricals. Coralie Mix Converse

**ONE FRIEND SAID OF MOLLIE FLY
(SHOWN HERE, CIRCA 1885):
"SHE WAS 5 FEET OF PURE DIGNITY AND BEAUTY."**

organized construction of a theater at Camp Lincoln. Historian Munson called it a remarkable accomplishment, given the site's isolation. Soldiers finished construction on the theater before completing their own quarters. Opening night drew settlers from 60 miles around.

Angeline Brown, a teacher in Prescott, conducted Sunday services that became popular among the town's gambling-house owners. "They always dressed in black broadcloth suits with white shirts and a good deal of jewelry," recalled merchant Morris Goldwater. "When they learned of the song service . . . they would all close their games Sunday morning and go to church and listen to the music, and then put a contribution in the plate and walk out and begin their games again."

Gambling was considered a respectable profession in the frontier West, a way for men to make money at a time when jobs were scarce. But the dictates of convention constrained the pioneer woman's options for earning a living. She could teach,

**ATTORNEY SARAH HERRING SORIN
EPITOMIZED THE PIONEER'S INDIVIDUALITY.**

run a boarding house, take in laundry and sewing, or work as a domestic, but not much else.

Yet few women performed even those jobs, according to author Christiane Fischer. In the *Journal of the West* for July, 1977, she wrote that the percentage of Arizona Territory's female population over age 10 and gainfully employed was small — 5 per cent in 1880 and 9 per cent in 1890.

The norms governing the public behavior of women seem quaint now, but they were so strict that causing a scene was rather easy.

"The spectacle of two of the feminine population mounted astraddle with divided skirts, capped by sombreros, almost upset the equilibrium of Washington Street, Phoenix, recently," the *Coconino Sun* reported on May 10, 1884.

The same year, Tucson's *Arizona Daily Star* reported that the propensity of amorous reverends to hug female members of their congregations prompted a scientist to invent a corset equipped with a padlock and sharp-pointed spikes "around the usual path of a man's arms."

The paper predicted that the invention wouldn't work because it is "mighty tough for the men of the country to be broken of their hugging propensities by means of a loaded corset."

But even with constraints, some women excelled.

Students of Arizona history know of photographer C.S. Fly. His pictures of the characters who populated Tombstone in its heyday, and particularly his images from the Apache campaigns, form a lasting record. Less well known is his wife, Mary Edith Goodrich Fly, known as Mollie. An accomplished photographer in San Francisco before she married, Mollie was the person who taught her husband the picture-taking skill.

At a time when women photographers were rare, Mollie strolled the streets of Tombstone offering to take pictures for 35 cents. She was the one with the head for business, and during her husband's frequent absences, Mollie ran their Tombstone photo gallery. Her entrepreneurial efforts on his behalf helped preserve a vital pictorial history of the American West. After C.S. Fly's death in 1905, she published a collection of his work, titled *Scenes in Geronimo's Camp: The Apache Outlaw and Murderer*.

In January, 1893, Sarah Herring, a woman of "innate dignity," penciled her name into the ledger kept by the territory's Supreme Court, thus becoming Arizona's first female attorney.

The *Arizona Weekly Star*, under the headline, "The World Moves," called her a "genuine heroine":

"She has thrown down the gauntlet to the so-called sterner sex, in asserting the right of woman to enter the race of life on equal terms with man. It was a courageous step by a courageous lady, and henceforth many other of our young women will follow in her path."

Born in New York City in 1861, Sarah moved to Tombstone at the height of the mining boom to watch her father, prominent atttorney William Herring, practice law.

Sarah was among the town's first schoolteachers and rose to school principal, but eventually followed in her father's footsteps. She graduated fourth in her class at New York University law school, and went into partnership with him, specializing in mining law. The firm was called Herring and Sorin, a last name she adopted professionally after her marriage to Thomas Sorin, a mine executive.

In the early 1900s, Sarah became the 25th woman to argue a case before the U.S. Supreme Court. But she also was known as a staunch opponent of women's suffrage. As one observer noted, "She appeared to look on her activity as a woman lawyer as something entirely different from the participation of women in lawmaking and elections."

Sarah was attorney for Globe's Old Dominion Copper Company when she died of pneumonia in 1914.

Cordelia Kay, the "Lady Miner of Mineral Park," made her mark as a businesswoman, scoring big strikes in gold, silver, and turquoise in the mountains of Mohave County. "The tenderfoot may think we mean that she hired the work done, but not so," wrote one newspaper. "Mrs. Kay cut the fuse, bit the cap, tamped the powder and returned into the smoke to see the result of the shot."

Elizabeth Hudson Smith moved to Wickenburg in 1897 and found work as a cook. Her food was so good that in 1905 the Santa Fe Railroad asked her to build a hotel for railway travelers. Her establishment, the Hotel Vernetta, was the town's first two-story building, and Elizabeth, a black woman, became one of Wickenburg's leading lights. She sponsored live dramas in the hotel's backyard, never charging admission. She taught French classes for women from as far away as Phoenix.

Mary Katharine Harony, better known as Big Nosed Kate, is remembered mainly for her love affair with the tubercular dentist Doc Holliday and her association with Wyatt Earp.

On her own from age 15, this Hungarian-born girl roamed the West, doing what was necessary to survive, including selling herself in such rough districts as Las Vegas, N.M.; Wichita, Kansas; and Deadwood, South Dakota.

And if surviving meant torching a hotel in Fort Griffin, Texas, to save Holliday from the hangman, so be it.

She did that in 1877, shortly before showing up in

REPLETE WITH PLUMED HAT AND STYLISH RIDING GARB, MINER CORDELIA KAY SITS ASTRIDE HER HORSE.

Tombstone as a side player in the Earp-Clanton drama. But Kate refused to live in Tombstone. She went to Globe, put down $500 to buy her own hotel, and became a successful madam.

Her last stop was the Arizona Pioneers' Home in Prescott, which had a policy against admitting foreigners. So Kate lied about her birthplace and got in, another sidestep in a life that can only be described as a cunning triumph.

She died in 1940, at age 89, and rests on the grounds of the Pioneers' Home under a marker that reads "Mary K. Cummings," one of her many aliases.

The frontier prostitute was a businesswoman of sorts, and a few prostitutes did quite well, especially after moving into management. Jennie Bauters ran a popular house in Jerome and accumulated considerable property before relocating to Mohave County. She owned a saloon and earned respect for her generosity to down-on-their-luck miners and prospectors. Jennie was murdered in 1905 in Gold Road.

Her shocking death so riled the citizenry that it prompted

the newspaper *Our Mineral Wealth* to publish this editorial blast at her murderer, who attempted suicide after the killing:

"The vampire having a shot left fired it into his own worthless body looking for a heart, but the bullet could only find the meat of a murderer. He will live to vex his keepers until the official rope shuts off the breath that some good mother gave him."

Call it sophisticated or call it shameful, but a prostitute was often semi-revered, at least by men. She performed a valuable function — keeping the lid on in mine towns where the work was so brutal it could bend a man's spine, and the grime on his neck was graveyard permanent.

Caroline Cedarholm knew nothing about life in an Arizona mine town in 1870, but she learned quickly. She was a Norwegian missionary, based in San Francisco, who believed God had called her to establish a Protestant church in Prescott. But Cedarholm found herself in Los Angeles with no money and no way of making passage to Arizona. So she stuffed her belongings into two bundles, balanced one on her head, and started on foot for Prescott, more than 400 miles away.

"The road was very hard, and I went on painfully, sometimes weeping and sometimes singing," she wrote later.

After getting rides here and there, and fighting off the advances of an amorous freighter, she reached her destination. But Cedarholm, and a missionary who had arrived earlier, found Prescott more interested in whiskey than salvation.

"Sometimes our zeal led us to go into the saloons and speak, which caused much opposition," she wrote.

For Nampeyo, a potter from the First Mesa village of Hano, personal zeal led to a different path. She was born about 1860, and her artistic brilliance helped revive a prehistoric pottery style known as Sikyatki.

She started out displaying her work at reservation trading posts. Her pots sold well, but Nampeyo sought to push her art beyond the standard of the day. She and her husband, Lesou, gathered and studied pottery shards from ancient sites, including the ruin of Sikyatki.

VISIONARY HOPI POTTER NAMPEYO, SURROUNDED BY HER ART, BURNISHES ONE OF HER POTS WITH A STONE.

At her induction into the Arizona Women's Hall of Fame, Nampeyo was described as an innovator who shared her techniques with other potters. Her craftsmanship made Nampeyo something of a celebrity at the turn of the century. The Santa Fe Railway Exhibition displayed her work twice in Chicago, in 1898, and 1919, and she demonstrated her skill for tourists at Fred Harvey's Hopi House at the Grand Canyon. He considered her the best potter in the Southwest.

Nampeyo went blind in 1920, but continued her pottery work with Lesou's help. She died in 1942, but her work and her inspiration is still felt among the Hopi.

Elizabeth Heiser possessed no capacity to please any part of the public. She was blunt, with a manner of speaking that, according to one recollection, carried "a strong smack of the soil and of the corral." Circumstance forced these on her, the same dynamic that guided the lives of every pioneer woman.

She and her husband arrived in Arizona from Buffalo, New York, in 1890, intending to start a cattle ranch, with Elizabeth as a traditional wife and housekeeper. The plan went awry when Charles Heiser became an invalid, and Elizabeth was forced into a role for which she was completely unprepared. But she was tough enough to pull it off.

For 30 years, she ran a successful ranch at Red Horse Tank, near Flagstaff. Elizabeth wore a pistol on her hip and could ride and shoot with any man. One winter, when severe weather threatened to kill her horses, she drove her herd to the bottom of the Grand Canyon and stayed until spring.

In 1916, the Heisers took in 13-year-old Thor Fitzgerald as their foster son, and five years later the family moved to Pasadena. In 1933, a year after Charles' death, Elizabeth made a splash in newspapers throughout California by marrying her fosterling. She was 65 and Thor 29, by then a Navy seaman who had to arrange shore leave the day of the wedding.

Elizabeth had extensive property holdings in Arizona and California and this led to whispers that Thor had married her to get rich. But Joe Meehan, director of the Arizona Historical Society in Flagstaff, doesn't believe that. For several years prior to Fitzgerald's death in 1994 at age 90, Meehan traded letters and phone calls with the old sailor and became convinced that Thor's affection for Elizabeth was genuine.

"He never remarried after she died, and by everything he said, you could tell it was a marriage of love," Meehan said. "I have no doubt about that."

Of course, Elizabeth couldn't have cared less what anyone said. She was her own woman.

She lost her left eye in 1895, when a doctor spilled alcohol on it while treating a cold. Elizabeth concealed the empty socket with a frosted lens that gave her a ghostly appearance. She kept the eye in a jar of formaldehyde, and Thor buried it with her when she died in 1947.

Her diary entry for February 9, 1895, is emblematic of the pioneer woman, how she accepted her fate, no matter how awful or unjust, without pity or explanation. Elizabeth wrote: "Had my eye cut out today by Dr. Cotton."

Mary Bernard Aguirre

*One feels awe at what she endured and
accomplished. She heard the "screams and
general uproar" of a Civil War battle as her first
son was born. When she was 25 and had three
children, Apache Indians killed her husband. She
persisted, becoming a frontier teacher and head
of two departments at the University of Arizona.*

———◆———

I N THE SPRING OF 1876, MARY BERNARD AGUIRRE WAS TEACH-
ing in the San Pedro River settlement of Tres Alamos, 30
miles east of Tucson, when a large Apache Indian appeared
outside the schoolhouse door. The sight caused a chorus of
wailing among Mary's students, and with good reason. Apache
bands still controlled much of southern Arizona, and many
killed with impunity.

Six years earlier, Mary's husband, Epifanio, and three
others were killed in an Apache raid on a stagecoach at Sasabe,
Arizona. And the schoolhouse where she taught once had be-
longed to a settler who also was killed by Indians. He left no
heirs, so officials appropriated the one-room adobe as a school.
It had a fireplace, a sash window, and a door that locked with
a key.

But on this day Mary was late arriving, and in her rush
she left the key outside. One of her students, a boy named
Eddie, spotted the Indian as he was arriving at school. He
screamed and accidentally turned the key, locking himself and
the mysterious Indian outside.

"The children looked like death they were so frightened,
and I, no less scared, called frantically to Eddie to unlock the

door," Mary wrote years later. "I suppose the Indian under-
stood for he unlocked and opened the door and poor Eddie
tumbled in, a limp heap, almost unconscious."

What seemed a threat turned into a comedy play. The
Indian strolled in, said "Good morning," and took a seat beside a girl, who gasped and rolled off the bench onto the floor.

By this time, Mary was laughing. She judged the Indian
to be harmless as he grabbed the girl's book and began flip-
ping the pages and looking at pictures.

The episode ended happily. But less than a week later,
when three members of a family living near present-day Benson
were slain by raiders, Mary learned that the charming visitor
was a warrior sent "to spy out the country and see how the
settlers were fixed with arms."

If that disturbing revelation alarmed Mary Aguirre, she
did not record it in her memoirs. But this isn't surprising. On
the frontier, life and death traveled like brethren, one at the
shoulder of the other, a link made so close by happenstance
an momentary fortune that talking about it would seem re-
dundant, even self-absorbed.

Mary was one of Tucson's first public school teachers, a
pillar in the town's educational foundation, and a true pioneer.
It would be hard to examine her life without feeling awe at
what she endured and what she saw.

She was born in St. Louis on June 23, 1844, and by age
12 was living in Westport, Missouri. Her father, Joab Bernard,
owned a thriving mercantile there, but material comforts could-
n't insulate them from social turmoil. The great debate over
slavery was exploding, and young Mary saw men marching at
night through the streets, beating drums and making war cries.

In the coming years she would witness many momentous events. While attending school in Baltimore in 1859, she
heard the rifle fire announcing the death of abolitionist John
Brown at Harpers Ferry, West Virginia. The following year she
returned to Westport, and when the Civil War came in 1861, she
became an ardent backer of the Southern cause.

MARY BERNARD AGUIRRE, WHOSE RINGLETS, EARRINGS, AND LACE COLLAR BELIE HER TOUGH, ADVENTURESOME SPIRIT.

"My first active recollection of this is helping to make the first Confederate flag in Missouri," said Mary, whose mother owned two slaves, marriage gifts from her parents.

The war brought hell to Westport. Homes of Southern sympathizers were burned. Men were shot in the streets. When rumors flew that a skirmish was about to erupt, the Bernard children took refuge in the family outhouse. They called it Fort Bell, after Mary's mother's maiden name.

"Still, for all this," Mary wrote, "youth will find pleasure. We had our rides and picnics occasionally, and we had happy times for all. We picked lint and tore bandages to send south, and studied and played the piano."

Even the birth of her first son, Pedro, in June, 1863, was tainted by the war. As Mary lay in labor, she listened to the "screams and general uproar" of a battle under way near Westport. She had two more sons, Epifanio and Stephen.

Many of her married years were taken up with travel, due largely to husband Epifanio's work freighting supplies to government posts. She came to the Southwest for the first time in the fall of 1863, making an epic three-month journey from Missouri to Santa Fe and down to Las Cruces, New Mexico. The trek is beautifully described in Mary's journal, held by the Arizona Historical Society. She marveled at the vastness of the land and the size of the buffalo that roamed the Great Plains.

"I can never forget the first one I ever saw," she wrote. "It had just been killed and we rode to where it was off of the road. I had a curiosity to measure the hair on the neck, which I did with my arm, and it covered from my fingertips to the shoulder."

When the party reached Santa Fe, they met John Noble Goodwin and traveled to Arizona with him. He was leading a party to establish Arizona Territory's first government. Mary Aguirre also witnessed the arrival in the New Mexico capital of 7,000 Navajo Indians. They'd been defeated in battle by Kit Carson and were about to embark on their "long walk" to the new reservation at Bosque Redondo.

Another trip, this one hauling wheat from Las Cruces to Fort Grant, brought Mary to Tucson for the first time in August, 1869. When husband Epifanio was killed five months later, she returned, disconsolate, to her family in Missouri. But she came back to Tucson in 1875 and took the teaching job in Tres Alamos.

Living conditions were primitive. She stayed in a small room at the back of a large, single-room adobe home owned by Thomas Dunbar. It served as post office, stage station, and sleeping quarters for travelers moving between Forts Bowie, Grant, and Apache. Lumber was scarce, so the floor of Mary's room had no boards. Only a blanket hanging in the doorway separated her quarters from the main house.

Her school had no seats, desks, or even a table. She did have a few pencils, a half-dozen beginning instruction books, and one high stool. Every morning, Mary walked a mile across the valley to the schoolhouse to teach. She sat on the stool, her feet dangling above the ground, and 23 students curled up on the dirt in front of her. Their desks were boards thrown across candle boxes.

Even so, Mary loved the job, her first as a teacher — until Apache terror again intervened in her life.

Word of the raid that killed a man and his two sons came before daylight on a Sunday. A rider going from ranch to ranch galloped up to the Dunbar home shouting, "Los Indios!" Within minutes, Mary and the Dunbars were shivering in their night-clothes, listening to the story of the killings, six miles away.

The fear intensified that night when a stage driver brought word that Indians had killed yet another settler near Fort Bowie. But even amid the troubles, Mary's journal documents a good bit of humor.

As the stage driver barked the news to the Dunbars, Mary was with another woman, identified only as Mrs. W. She'd left her husband at their home near Cienega Creek and was an overnight guest of the Dunbars. The two women stood at the doorway to Mary's room, riveted by every word. Someone asked which way the Indians headed after the Bowie killing. "They went towards the Cienega!" the driver said.

Mrs. W. began screaming in a most awful way that her husband was dead. "It was like bedlam let loose," Mary wrote. "Mrs. W. fell down in a sort of fit and kicked the door and carried on dreadful." Her hollering was so loud that the stage driver, who'd been sitting on the door sill, leaped and exclaimed, "Good Lord, what's that?!"

"I'm quite sorry to remember," Mary wrote, "that I put my head on my pillow and laughed most shamefully when I heard that man jump off the door sill."

In that night's mail, Mary received a letter from her brother in Tucson telling her not to return to the schoolhouse and to sit tight because he was coming to get her. "So my first school was broken up by Indians," she wrote.

After returning to Tucson in May of 1876, Mary was appointed replacement teacher at the Tucson Public School for Girls. A month remained in the term and she had 20 students in her charge. Again, her journal gives a vivid account of the experience:

"With a few exceptions, they were the most unruly set the Lord ever let live. They had an idea that they conferred a favor upon the school and teacher by attending. . . . The recess bell was a signal for those girls to climb out of the windows into the street, to whoop and scream like mad."

Mary allowed the first recess to pass, and in the afternoon refused to allow a single girl to leave her seat. The students grumbled, but stayed put on penalty of being sent home. Over the days, some girls refused to show up and others were ordered home for various infractions. By the end of the first week, when Arizona Governor A.P.K. Safford came to visit, Mary had five students remaining. He asked how she was getting along and got an earful.

"Governor, I have about broken up your girl's school trying to keep order," Mary lectured. "Unless I can have order I would not teach this school for five hundred dollars a month."

Safford laughed until his eyes teared up, and said, "Mrs. Aguirre, you just go on breaking up the school that way. You shall keep this school if you never have more than five scholars." But the students soon returned, and they numbered 40 when school closed at month's end.

The rebellion of her students was fueled by Catholic opposition to public schooling. It was the day's hot issue. Because a local judge and several Tucson priests spoke vehemently against it, many upper-class Mexican families refused to let their girls attend, and those who did were ostracized.

But Mary's reputation changed that. She was so well

known and respected throughout Arizona and Sonora that when she took charge of the school, Mexican families began sending their girls to her. Even the nieces of the priest who'd preached most sternly against the school began attending. "That settled the matter," Mary wrote. "But my troubles in the first year were many and sore."

She kept the job for three years, relinquishing it only when her health failed. At her resignation in 1879, the school had 85 girls. Mary's work in education continued in 1895 when she became head of the Spanish language and English history departments at the University of Arizona.

To students of irony, her death in California in 1906 provided much to ponder. The woman who'd survived thousands of miles of travel across thoroughly wild land, on horseback, on foot, and atop tons of wheat stuffed into the hold of a huge prairie-schooner wagon, suffered fatal injuries while riding in a plush Pullman car.

She was on her way to San Jose for the summer when her train jumped the tracks and flipped over. Mary was hurled against a seat, and another passenger landed on top of her. Her brother, N.W. Bernard, the same one who'd summoned her from Tres Alamos 30 years before, rushed from Tucson to keep a vigil at her bedside. She held on for two weeks, finally succumbing to internal injuries on May 24, 1906. She was 61.

Sarah Bowman

*Her size — more than 6 feet tall and
200 pounds — earned her the nickname
"the Great Western." As a civilian cook for the
Army, her bravery under fire brought accolades
and headlines from around the country.
Her work running tent kitchens, saloons, and
brothels for soldiers won her their
lasting admiration.*

———⟫•⟪———

EW WOMEN LEFT BIGGER FOOTPRINTS ON THE FRONTIER
than Sarah Bowman. From the Mexican War of 1846
to her later years in Yuma and Patagonia in Arizona —
running tent kitchens, saloons, and brothels for soldiers —
she was a startling presence. The diaries and memoirs of the
men who knew her describe a hurricane of a personality, a sexual libertine, shrewd businesswoman, and big-hearted soul
who cared for men in a "motherly" way.

In various accounts, she is depicted as having reddish
hair, a fair complexion, blue eyes, and often with two pistols
bouncing on her hips. This "giantess," perhaps of Irish de-
scent, weighed about 200 pounds and, in the words of soldier-
memoirist George Washington Trahern, "could whip most
anybody in a rough-and-tumble fight." Her nickname was "the
Great Western," after an enormous side-wheeler steamship of
the late 1830s, appropriate considering that Trahern's memoirs
described her as "immense."

Much of Sarah's life sounds like legend and, indeed, some
stories told about her cannot be tracked to factual sources.
Even her background is hazy. The federal census for 1860 lists

her birthplace as Tennessee, but Sarah's burial certificate says that she was born in Clay County, Missouri, in 1813. Author J.F. Elliott, in a profile published in 1989 in the *Journal of Arizona History*, wrote that she was illiterate, had at least three husbands, and took countless other men into her blankets. He believes these liasons almost surely produced children, although no records exist.

Sarah first came into public view, around 1840, after she and her husband enlisted in the 8th Infantry at Jefferson Barracks in St. Louis. As a cook and laundress, she accompanied the unit to Florida during the Seminole War. When hostilities with Mexico flared in 1845, she stuffed her tents and cooking gear into a donkey cart and marched with Gen. Zachary Taylor's forces west along the Rio Grande River from Corpus Christi, Texas.

In March, 1846, Taylor's men dug in on the American side of the river opposite Matamoros, building an earthen fort. On May 1, Taylor rode to Port Isabel on the Gulf of Mexico to secure his supply line, leaving behind some 50 men to guard the position, later called Fort Brown. Two days later, the Mexicans began shelling with 8-pound cannon. The bombardment continued for the next 160 hours.

The women of the fort were ordered to shelter, but Sarah refused to go. She continued to cook, and even serve coffee to the men along the walls, as the shells flew. Historian Arthur Woodward wrote that she worked "with the utmost coolness and disdain of the Mexican copper shot and cannon balls that buzzed and banged in all directions."

One bullet passed through her bonnet, and another crashed into a bread tray she was carrying.

In the midst of it all, she helped make cartridges and tend the wounded. When word spread that the Mexicans were set to charge, she grabbed a musket and prepared to fight. An artillery officer later toasted her, saying that "her bravery was the admiration of all who were in the fort."

With newspapers around the country hailing Sarah as

SARAH BOWMAN'S GRAVESTONE.

the heroine of Fort Brown, Taylor's troops marched into Mexico, stopping at Saltillo, where Sarah operated the American House hotel. As with every stop she made, her actions were colorful and often remarked upon. Sam Curtis, of the 3rd Ohio Volunteers, wrote in his journal: "She had several servants, Negro and Mexican, and she knocks them about like little children."

At the battle of Buena Vista, fought near Saltillo on February 23, 1847, an American soldier fled in panic when the Mexicans attacked. Memoirist Trahern describes the soldier running all the way to Sarah's place in Saltillo, screaming that Taylor was whipped out. "The Great Western" was horrified. "She just drew off and hit him between the eyes and knocked him sprawling," wrote Trahern. " 'You damned son of a bitch, there ain't Mexicans enough to whip old Taylor. You just spread that report and I'll beat you to death.' "

Capt. George Lincoln, who had enlisted Sarah and her first husband at St Louis, died in the same battle. Writer G.N.

Allen said that she "fell upon a chair and wept like a child" at the news.

"Poor dear man, I must go and see to him this very night," Sarah said, "lest them rascally greasers should strip him, and not knowing him, I could not give him a decent burial." She fetched Captain Lincoln's body and buried him at Saltillo.

In 1848, while following Taylor's troops, she married a soldier whose name is uncertain, but probably was Charles Bourgette. He must have died before departing Mexico, because in July of that year, when she tried to travel home with the 2nd Dragoons, Maj. Daniel Rucker said no — unless she married one of the enlisted men and was mustered in as a laundress.

"All right, Major," Sarah said, "I'll marry the whole squadron and you thrown in, but what I go along."

She rode past the line of soldiers and cried, "Who wants a wife with $15,000 and the biggest leg in Mexico? Come, me beauties, don't all speak at once. Who is the lucky man?"

After a long wait, a soldier named Davis stepped forward and said he'd be her husband if a clergyman married them. Sarah roared in laughter. "Bring your blanket to my tent tonight and I will learn you to tie a knot that will satisfy you, I reckon."

The relationship didn't last. Before long, Sarah spotted a handsome soldier bathing and "conceived a violent passion for his gigantic proportions," according to *My Confession*, a book by ex-soldier Sam Chamberlain.

"The Sampson . . . became the willing captive to this modern Delilah," Chamberlain wrote, "who straightaway kicked Davis out of her affections and tent, and established her elephantine lover in full possession without further ceremony."

Sarah landed in El Paso in 1849, briefly operated a hotel, and became the town's first prostitute of record. She turned up next in Socorro, New Mexico. According to author Brian Sandwich, her most recent biographer, the federal census for Socorro lists her as living with five orphan children, all named Skinner, that she probably adopted on the trip to El Paso. She also had a new husband, 24-year-old Albert Bowman, a sergeant in the 2nd Dragoons. Sarah stayed with this upholsterer, miner, and carpenter for 16 years, longer than any other man.

After Albert's discharge, he and Sarah moved to Fort Yuma, Calif., arriving late in 1852. When Arizona City, later renamed Yuma, was laid out across the river from the fort in 1854, Sarah became the town's first permanent Anglo resident. Her house, built at the corner of Main and First streets, became a sutler's store for troops. But she was never sold on the town, once describing it as "separated from hell by one thin sheet of sandpaper."

The best information about her time in Yuma comes from the diary of Samuel P. Heintzelman, Fort Yuma's commander, and the letters of Sylvester Mowry, an officer stationed at the fort in the 1850s. Heintzelman's relationship with Sarah was complicated and contentious. At varying times, he consorted with her, did business with her, expressed jealousy at her sexual romps, complained about the food she served officers, and was even used by her.

In the spring of 1854, she approached Heintzelman with a problem concerning two of her orphan girls. She explained that unnamed people from San Diego, apparently suspicious that she was putting her charges to work in the bordello, were coming to take them from her. She wished to move across the river to Mexico to escape them.

"She took them when they were left destitute," wrote Heintzelman in his diary, "and has been a mother to them and is attached to them and they to her. . . . I do not believe anyone could take them from her."

Sarah never explained why anyone in distant San Diego would care about the possible sexual activities of two orphan girls. Her story was likely a ploy to get the Army's help in setting up another hotel-brothel. Heintzelman provided the assistance and visited the house during its construction. "I can't see what she expects to do for a living when she moves over there," he wrote dimly.

STEAMSHIPS AND FREIGHTERS AT FORT YUMA.

When he saw girls coming and going from Sarah's new digs, the major realized he had been played for a fool. In one instance, Heintzelman described a "peon" girl who, seeking to join Sarah across the river, "stripped all to her petticoats and got astride a balsa [log] and clasped it with her arms whilst an Indian pushed her across." The strange incident angered Heintzelman: "I am very provoked at that strumpet."

But within a few days of writing those words, he was at Sarah's place, and it sounds as if his boots were off: "We all went across the river . . . on the Western's invitation. It helped pass the day."

At Yuma, as elsewhere, Sarah proved herself a first-rate promoter who "never missed an opportunity in business," wrote Sandwich in his 1991 biography, *The Great Western*. She used whatever trick was necessary to secure the mess contract, and was wise enough to cater to officers making $70 to $80 per month, rather than buck privates making $7. She also was keenly aware of what made men tick.

Mowry, in a letter to relatives, wrote: "I have just got a little Sonoran [Mexican] girl for a mistress. She is seventeen, very pretty. . . . For the present she is living with the Great

Western and comes up nights to my room. . . . Among her [Sarah's] other good qualities, she is an admirable pimp."

Even Yuma's priest, Father Paul Figueroa, could find nothing to criticize, calling Sarah "a good-hearted woman, good soul, old lady of great experience."

In the fall of 1856, Sarah and Albert moved to Tucson to open a boarding house.

On the way they passed the site of the Oatman massacre and stopped to move the family's remains from a loose rock pile to more permanent graves beside the Gila Trail. Earlier that year, when Olive Oatman returned to Fort Yuma after five years in captivity, Sarah took her in and cared for her, and Sandwich believes a bond was formed.

Sarah's last stint with the army came in 1857. She and Albert sold their property in Tucson and accompanied the 1st Dragoons to Sonoita Creek, in southeast Arizona, to establish Fort Buchanan. Sarah ran a saloon and whorehouse in nearby Patagonia.

Jeff Ake, whose father worked cutting hay for the troops, remembered her years later: "She packed two six-shooters, and they all said she shore could use 'em, that she had killed a couple of men in her time. She was a hell of a good woman."

When the fort was abandoned at the start of the Civil War, she moved out, sending "her girls back to Mexico where they came from."

Sarah spent her last years back in Yuma. Elliott says she was there in 1862 when the California Column came through to reclaim Tucson from Confederates. Even at that late stage of her life — she was about 49 — she wanted to travel with the troops. But that was no longer allowed. At some point during this period, her marriage to Albert dissolved, and he remarried in 1864.

The cause of Sarah's death, on December 23, 1866, is unknown, although one source says that she died from the bite of a poisonous spider. With the 12th Infantry band playing, and soldiers keeping step, her flag-draped casket was marched across the river and buried, with a rifle salute, in the cemetery at Fort Yuma. Sarah Boman was the only woman so honored.

Twenty-four years later, in the summer of 1890, her remains, and those of 159 soldiers, were dug up and moved to the Presidio National Cemetery in San Francisco. When workers opened the grave of the woman known as "the greatest whore in the West," the most tangible artifact they found was an unusually large medallion of the kind usually worn by Roman Catholics.

CHAPTER THREE

Nellie Cashman

*She cared for down-on-their-luck miners and
raised money to build churches and hospitals.
She brought conscience, charity, and decency
to wild settlements where the only "ethic"
was the fever to get rich. Her charitable nature
disguised other traits that made her
a tough, aggressive prospector and miner,
willing to compete with anyone.*

O F ALL THE REMARKABLE FACTS IN THE LIFE OF NELLIE Cashman, none stands out more than this: Her reputation was pure. In nearly 80 years of hard living — much of it as a boomtown miner from frontier Arizona to Alaskan tent camps — she made no significant enemies. Instead, praise, acclaim, and awe attached to her freely as dust from Tombstone's Allen Street.

It seems impossible for anyone to earn such a legacy. Surely Nellie was a Milquetoast who seldom uttered a discouraging word. Consider some of her comments from an interview with Bernice Cosulich of *The Arizona Daily Star* in December, 1923.

• On women in business: "Some women . . . think they should be given special favors because of their sex. Well, all I can say is that those special favors spell doom to a woman and her business. . . . I've paid my bills and played the game like a man."

• On seeing Los Angeles for the first time: "What dump is this? The city of angels? There was nothing, absolutely nothing, but dogs in sight. It was the first time I knew that dogs had souls."

• On the opposite sex: "Men. Why, child, they're just boys grown up. I've nursed them, embalmed them, fed and scolded them, acted as mother confessor . . . and you have to treat them just like boys."

Actually, one negative did follow Nellie Cashman: She spoke her mind, an uncommon trait among 19th-century women. But the criticism paled next to the work she did — feeding, housing, and caring for down-on-their-luck miners and raising money to build churches and hospitals. She brought conscience, charity, and decency to wild settlements, where the only "ethic" was the fever to get rich.

But Nellie had the fever, too. California author Don Chaput, Cashman's biographer, defined her character best when he wrote that her good works "have tended to disguise what she really was, a tough, aggressive prospector and miner, willing to compete with anyone, in any place, for the golden and silver harvest."

Nellie was always sinking new shafts and grubstaking miners in the hope of making the big score. Some say she turned over two or three fortunes in her lifetime. But the money never stayed long in her pocket, and if it wasn't enough to mend the shattered legs of a miner who had tumbled down a shaft, she went out and scrounged for more.

"If she asked for a contribution, we contributed," wrote John P. Clum, founder of the *Tombstone Epitaph* and a friend of Cashman's from her Arizona days. "And although Nellie's pleas were frequent, none ever refused her."

Ellen "Nellie" Cashman was 34 when she left Tucson to join the Tombstone silver rush, but her reputation as a frontier angel was already forming. She was born in 1845 near Queenstown, in County Cork, Ireland, and, according to Chaput, came to the United States with her sister, Fanny, and widowed mother, Frances, probably in 1850. The family traveled to San Francisco about 1865.

Nine years later, she took part in the gold rush to the Cassiar Mountains of Canada's British Columbia. She opened

NELLIE CASHMAN AS A SERENE YOUNG WOMAN.

a boarding house for miners and tapped her customers for donations to help the Sisters of St. Anne, in nearby Victoria, build a hospital. That winter, while in Victoria delivering $500 to the nuns, Nellie received word that Cassiar miners had been cut off by fierce snows and were suffering from scurvy. She organized a party of six men, collected hundreds of pounds of provisions, and set out in the dead of winter to rescue them.

The local army commander, believing that such a midwinter rescue effort was evidence of insanity, sent soldiers to bring them back.

"The guard found her encamped on the ice of Stickeen [River] cooking her evening meal by the heat of a wood fire and humming a lively air," reported the *Victoria Daily British Colonist*. "So happy, contented and comfortable did she appear that the 'boys in blue' sat down and took tea at her invitation."

The rescue party continued on for 77 days, fighting through bitter mountain weather, with Nellie pulling her own sled the entire way. When finally at the side of the sick men, she put them on a diet rich in vitamin C and stayed to ensure that they stuck to it. Some credit her with saving 75 lives.

Nellie lived by the same code in Tombstone. If a need existed, she filled it. She was instrumental in raising money to build Sacred Heart Catholic Church, and she used her contacts with the Sisters of St. Joseph in Tucson, and other orders, to secure nursing help for the new Cochise County hospital.

In the summer of 1881, Nellie's brother-in-law died, leaving her sister, Fanny, with five children. Nellie insisted that the family come to Arizona to live. Fanny died in Tombstone two years later, leaving Nellie with the daunting task of raising the kids, ages 5 to 12. She did so without flinching.

But the responsibility didn't diminish Nellie's desire for adventure. In the spring of 1883, word spread through Tombstone of a great gold field on Mexico's Baja California Peninsula. With Nellie as its leader, a party of 21 men headed for Mexico. It included some of the town's most prominent citizens, such as Marcus A. Smith, who went on to become a Territorial delegate to Congress and an Arizona senator, and Milt Joyce, owner of the Oriental Saloon.

Chaput reports that after a difficult sailing trip to Trinidad Bay, the group still had 100 miles to go. Nellie decided to lead five or six men ahead to the placer fields, with the main party to come later. But the heat was ferocious, greater than anything they'd known in Arizona, and within 16 hours their water supply was almost gone.

"They stopped, boiled in the sun, and were about to become ex-miners," wrote Chaput. Stories of their rescue vary, but it's probable that they were saved by Mexicans returning from the fields who came upon Nellie "nearly dead from exhaustion." The expedition earned her an untimely obituary when the *Phoenix Herald* misreported that she and two others had died of thirst.

Later that year, according to Clum, she was in the middle of one of the West's dramatic hangings. A botched robbery in

Bisbee in December, 1883, left several bystanders dead. Five of the perpetrators were to hang in the yard behind the Tombstone courthouse on March 28, 1884. So many citizens wanted to see the hangings that Sheriff J.L. Ward ran out of official passes. A local carpenter built a grandstand in the lot adjacent to the courthouse and planned to charge admission.

Nellie had been visiting regularly with the condemned men, and in Clum's words, "her Celtic soul was stained with indignation" that their deaths were being turned into a holiday. She convinced the chief of police to issue a curfew on execution eve, keeping mobs off the street. Then, in darkness, she marched to the grandstand with some miners carrying sledgehammers and axes.

The citizens of Tombstone awoke to a surprise. "They discovered that the grandstand had been reduced to a mass of kindling wood and deposited at the bottom of a convenient arroyo," Clum wrote in his book, *Nellie Cashman, Angel of the Camp*.

But Nellie's work wasn't done. When rumors spread that the bodies of the executed killers would be sold as cadavers to a medical school, she arranged for two prospectors to spend 10 nights camped at the Boothill graveyard to ensure that the corpses remained undisturbed.

Asked late in life if she'd ever been frightened by her frontier adventures, Nellie said: "I was never afraid of anything. I figure I have too much to do to be afraid."

In Tombstone, those who troubled Nellie were the ones who needed to be afraid. One published report tells of a diner at Russ House, the building that housed Nellie's combination restaurant/hotel, fussing about the quality of her beans. A man at an adjoining table (Doc Holliday in some accounts) drew a sidearm, pointed it at the complainer, and asked him to repeat his assessment of the proprietor's cooking. "Best I ever ate," his hapless target croaked.

It sounds like legend, but it shows the esteem in which she was held.

DIGNIFIED IN FEATHERED HAT AND SPECTACLES, NELLIE CASHMAN STILL LIVED A VIGOROUS LIFE OF ADVENTURE INTO HER OLD AGE.

Yet Nellie also was an enigma. She had an infectious Irish charm, a powerful brogue, and a foghorn laugh that seemed improbable coming from a slender woman of barely 5 feet. The memoirs of pioneers who knew her and reporters who interviewed her invariably note her good looks, particularly the dark, lustrous eyes, and remark with some wonder that she never married, although she seemed to enjoy the company of men.

One story described Nellie responding to a joke, saying that she "thwacked her knee and laughed like a boy." Writers found it comforting, following mention of her bachelorhood or her physical prowess, to point out some trait of hers considered more feminine.

In the *Arizona Daily Star*, October 24, 1885, we read that she rode 60 miles on horseback from Casa Grande to Tucson, "a jaunt that would nearly have prostrated the average man with fatigue." Later, the writer reassures us with this observation: "What Miss Cashman's age is may be a subject of conjecture. She is perhaps as sensitive concerning it as any other woman."

The trouble with attempting to pigeonhole Nellie is exactly the opposite: She was unlike any other woman. She followed her own voices. Author Frank Brophy, who heard stories about Nellie from his father, a family friend, even suggested she was a mystic, one who communicated directly with God. It seems farfetched, but the size of her selflessness invites speculation that it derived from a source we cannot see.

After leaving Tombstone in 1886, Nellie continued the rambling life, and doing heaven's business. She ran restaurants or boarding houses in Nogales, Jerome, Prescott, Yuma, and Harqua Hala, west of Phoenix. In 1898, she joined the gold stampede to Alaska and the Yukon, spending seven years in Dawson operating a retail store and helping finance yet another hospital renovation. In one room of her store, known as the Prospectors Haven of Retreat, she served coffee and doled out free cigars to miners. When Dawson played out, it was on to Fairbanks and Nolan Creek, near the Arctic Circle, some of the roughest land on earth.

As an oddity and a celebrity, Nellie's name kept turning up in the papers. While visiting California in 1921, she told *Sunset* magazine she'd like to be appointed U.S. deputy marshal for Alaska's Koyukuk District.

"I've been through Alaska dozens of times," she said, "but I've never been troubled by bad men. There isn't a man in Alaska who doesn't take off his hat whenever he meets me — and they always stop swearing when I come round, too. I wouldn't have any trouble in keeping order."

The following year, the Associated Press news service reported on her extraordinary trip from Nolan Creek to Anchorage: "Miss Cashman mushed, that is to say, part of the time she ran behind a dog sled, and part of the time rode by standing on the runners, 750 miles in 17 days." She was nearly 79.

But Nellie's "amazing vitality," as Clum called it, finally broke, and she became seriously ill with pneumonia and rheumatism near her cabin at Nolan Creek. Friends took her to the same hospital in Victoria, operated by the Sisters of St. Anne, that she had helped build, with money collected from Cassiar miners, 51 years before.

Decades after her famous rescue mission, one of the miners she had saved from scurvy was on his deathbed when he said, "If Nellie Cashman were only here, I'd get well." Such are the dreams of the dying. We have no record of what Nellie might've dreamed on January 4, 1925, the day the angel returned home.

CHAPTER FOUR

Pauline Cushman

*She filled her life with adventures at a time when
genteelness was more the measure of women. As
a teenager living at a trading post in Michigan,
she learned to ride, shoot, and navigate canoes
over fierce rapids. Later, her service to the
Union Army as a spy earned her a respect that
regenerated three decades after the Civil War.*

—◦—

AULINE CUSHMAN WAS AN ACTRESS WHOSE TRUE DEEDS
dwarfed the ones she portrayed on stage. Her life was
her finest role, a medley of despair and triumph that
in many ways mirrored the American experience in the 19th
century. She was a federal spy, commissioned a major by
President Lincoln for her daring Civil War service. After the
war, she toured western theaters as a Union heroine, and rowdy
audiences responded by firing their pistols at the ceiling instead of applauding.

Cushman became famous. Her eyes were black, and she
had raven ringlets falling almost to her waist. She was known
to pack a pistol and a hard punch, and she used both during
her time as a boardinghouse operator in frontier Arizona.

But in the tradition of classic stage tragedies, Cushman's
life ended in a San Francisco flophouse. As one obituary put it,
she died "childless and gray-haired," full of morphine to dull the
pain of her last days.

Cushman was born in New Orleans on June 10, 1833.
After a business failure, her father, a Spaniard from Madrid,
moved the family to Grand Rapids, Michigan, where he operated
a trading post frequented by Chippewa Indians.

There, Pauline lived her first adventures. An early biographer presents her as the darling of the Chippewa tribe, soldiers, and others who came to her father's store to trade. Her admirers taught her to ride bareback, shoot, and skin game. It was said that she had the pluck to navigate a canoe over the fiercest rapids.

At 18 she went to New York and signed on with a theatrical troupe called the New Orleans Varieties. She was a fast success, landing a co-starring role in *The Seven Sisters*, playing opposite John McDonogh, described as the matinee idol of his day.

In 1863, the troupe traveled to Louisville, Kentucky, a city roiled by wartime passions and dark intrigue. The venue was perfect for Pauline.

As part of her role in *The Seven Sisters*, Pauline was required to toast the Union. But Southern sympathizers offered her a $300 bribe to hail Confederate President Jefferson Davis instead. She reported the offer to the federal commandant at Louisville. Together, they plotted to go ahead with the suggested toast and use the uproar it would surely cause as a cover for her new job as an operative for the Secret Service.

In her obituary on December 6, 1893, the *Arizona Daily Citizen* reported that Pauline mounted the stage at Wood's Theater the following night, and "while the eyes of a large audience were fixed upon her in a supper scene, she proposed this toast: 'Here's to Jeff Davis and the Southern Confederacy. May the South always maintain her honor and her rights.' "

The theater, packed with paroled Confederate officers and patriotic Unionists, exploded with rebel yells, jeers, and a few fistfights. The outraged theater manager fired Pauline.

Then she went to work, infiltrating Louisville's most active Confederate sectors. But her most dangerous assignment came in Nashville, headquarters of the North's Army of the Cumberland and its chief of Army police, William Truesdail.

He and Gen. William Rosecrans needed someone to go behind rebel lines and gather information on the strength of

Pauline Cushman

**PAULINE CUSHMAN RELISHED
REGALING HER AUDIENCES IN MILITARY UNIFORM.**

Gen. Braxton Bragg's forces around Shelbyville. They summoned Pauline, and she headed off under the guise of searching for her missing brother, who was, in fact, a rebel major on Bragg's staff.

Pauline's boldness nearly caused her death. In violation of Truesdail's orders, she made crude sketches of Confederate positions and stole documents from the desk of a Southern officer. With the information stuffed into her shoe, she began to make her way back to Union lines. But she was captured, escaped, and captured again.

She was sent to rebel Gen. Nathan Bedford Forrest, who reportedly said: "Miss Cushman, I'm glad to see you. You're pretty sharp at turning a card, but I think we have you on this last shuffle."

At Shelbyville, she was sentenced to die on the gallows,

but her life was spared when General Rosecrans attacked the city, and she was left behind as the rebels retreated.

Back in Nashville, Pauline became ill from her exertions, and she was attended by a warm-hearted Yankee general named James Garfield. This future president admired Pauline and wrote to Abraham Lincoln, detailing the bravery of the woman Union troops had dubbed "The Major."

"Let her keep the title," Lincoln wrote to Garfield. "She has done more to earn the title than many a male who wore the shoulder straps of a major during the war."

When her health improved, Pauline toured the nation's theaters in her uniform, reciting her war adventures to enthralled audiences and drawing six-gun salutes in response.

But in Pauline's life, success and sadness seemed to go hand in hand. Her first husband, Charles Dickinson, died of dysentery in 1862. Her two children by that marriage both died in childhood, and her second husband, August Fichtner, died shortly after their marriage in 1872.

Soon she was in love again, this time with Dr. Samuel Orr, an Army surgeon. But it was another ill-fated romance. In 1875, Orr was called for duty at Arizona's Fort Bowie, where he fell ill and died. These painful episodes didn't eliminate Cushman's penchant for adventure or quell her fiery temper. She kept making news.

She was managing a resort south of San Francisco called La Honda when she taught its owner, Bill Sears, a brutal lesson in manners. Sears' affections for Pauline were not returned, and he sought revenge by telling lies about her to anyone who would listen.

Pauline resigned her position, and on the morning of her departure, a crowd gathered to see her off. When Sears arrived to see about the commotion, Pauline approached the stage driver and took his six-horse whip. Dressed in a red velvet gown and a plumed hat, the famous actress lashed into Sears, striking him repeatedly.

According to one account, dust rose from Sears' clothing

after each crack of the whip. When she was finished, Pauline returned the whip to the driver and said, "Thank you, sir. It's a good whip."

But to Jeremiah Fryer, a handsome man of Cherokee blood, who was many years her junior, Pauline was considerably warmer. She married him on January 29, 1879, and together they bought a hotel and livery stable in Casa Grande, Arizona Territory.

The business thrived, thanks to the couple's hard work and the arrival, in 1880, of the Southern Pacific Railroad. This pushed Casa Grande's population well above the handful it had been when the Fryers arrived. It also gave Pauline, now known as Major Fryer, more targets for her temper. Area newspapers carried accounts such as this: "Major Fryer doused Mrs. Cunningham in the water trough for slander."

In a story published in the *Arizona Republican* in 1925, Charles Eastman described meeting Pauline Cushman Fryer when he arrived in Casa Grande in 1884. Pauline was "good-hearted and an excellent nurse in taking care of anyone injured by bullet wounds."

That almost included Eastman. One night he was wobbling down the street, drunk, when The Major asked if he had seen her "long-legged husband."

Eastman replied that he did not keep track of women's husbands. Cushman drew a .45, stuck it into Eastman's belly, and demanded an answer "due a lady."

Now unexpectedly sober, Eastman replied that he had not seen Mr. Fryer.

"That's the way to answer a lady," she remarked.

Eastman wrote that a mollified Pauline "to my great relief took the .45 away from my grub sack."

Eastman once witnessed a street duel in Casa Grande in which Pauline played the referee. A man named Price Johnson was killed by a man identified only as Robinson.

"During the shooting," Eastman remembered, "Major Fryer stood there on the corner, the bullets whistling within

AS AN ACTRESS, PAULINE CUSHMAN OFTEN PERFORMED IN SCANTY ATTIRE.

15 or 20 feet of where she was standing. At no time did she flinch."

Pauline displayed her bravery again in 1889 in Florence, Arizona, where the Fryers had moved after Jeremiah became sheriff of Pinal County. The sheriff was out of town when a band of vigilantes threatened to drag some prisoners from their cells and lynch them.

With a Winchester rifle on her lap, The Major plopped

down in her husband's chair in the jailhouse and calmly turned back the hotheads.

But by this time, Pauline's life was unraveling, She was spending more and more of her time tracking down her missing husband, whose rumored infidelities made her half-crazy.

Mike Rice, a hotel bellboy who befriended her in California in 1871, wrote that her extreme jealousy, coupled with an "inordinate infatuation" with her husband, forced her to "extraordinary methods to retain his waning affections."

Hearing of a woman from a nearby town who was about to become the mother of an unwanted baby, she conspired to acquire the infant and pass it off to Fryer as her own. She told her husband that she was pregnant and that she should give birth at a hospital in San Francisco. The pregnant woman, already in that city, gave birth to a girl who became Emma Pauline Fryer.

For a time, the plan worked. The marriage stabilized with little Emma at its center. But she was afflicted from birth with an incurable nervous disorder and suffered violent spasms. At age six she died. Shortly thereafter, Fryer learned of Pauline's desperate ruse, and the marriage was over.

In 1890, she returned to San Francisco, dusted off her major's uniform, and attempted to revive her post-Civil War recitals. She frittered away the last of her money living at the posh Baldwin Hotel, hoping that someone would notice that she was back in town.

But no one did. The war was long over, and Pauline had become a haggard 57-year-old has-been, a star without a galaxy.

Her last years were spent at a boarding house on San Francisco's Market Street, working as a scrubwoman and battling arthritis and rheumatism. A doctor gave her morphine tablets for pain, and early in December, 1893, the medicine killed her.

The official coroner's report stated that she died of a morphine overdose "taken without suicidal intent and to relieve pain."

Major Cushman's final hurrah befit a woman who flourished and suffered, along with her country, through the Civil War, the coming of the railroad, and the settling of the Western frontier.

In the days after her death, newspapers reported that The Major, whose end came amid abject poverty, would be buried in potter's field. An uproar ensued, led by the Grand Army of the Republic, an organization of war veterans.

Donations poured in to remedy the injustice. Her body was laid to rest in a "handsome cloth-covered casket" draped with an American flag, and she was given a military honor guard and a rifle salute.

The Major would've beamed at the attention and at the simple remembrance printed on her grave marker: "Pauline Cushman, Federal Spy and Scout of the Cumberland."

CHAPTER FIVE

Josephine "Sadie" Marcus Earp

After she arrived in raucous boomtown Tombstone as a teenage dancer in a traveling troupe, Josie first took up with Sheriff Johnny Behan and then with his foe, Wyatt Earp. The bitterness flowing from this romantic tangle contributed mightily to the West's most famous shoot-out, the gunfight in October, 1881, at the O.K. Corral.

———❖———

EARLY TOMBSTONE WAS PACKED WITH MEN WHO LIVED FOR the sizzle of the moment, and voluptuous, flirtatious Josephine "Sadie" Marcus was sizzle from head to toe. What a perfect match when Arizona's most storied boomtown and one of its most enigmatic women came together in 1880.

Much of what happened in the old silver camp, including the story of Wyatt Earp and the O.K. Corral fight, still is being examined amid a tangle of motivations, hatreds, and political machinations. But one aspect of the tale is blessedly simple: Josie's considerable charms sparked a competition between Wyatt and Cochise County sheriff's appointee Johnny Behan. Wyatt eventually won her heart, but the bitterness caused by the romantic rivalry was a principal cause of the West's most famous shoot-out.

"It was uproariously funny," wrote Frank Waters in *The Earps of Tombstone*, an angry anti-Earp book, "to see the politically affluent governor's appointee as sheriff risking his office and reputation to chase Sadie down the back alleys. It

**THIS BADLY CREASED PHOTO SHOWS JOSIE EARP
WITH AN ELDERLY WYATT UNDER A CANVAS RAMADA.**

was pathetically tragic to watch the future national TV hero lusting mightily after the same chit of a girl."

Who was this headstrong woman at the center of the legend? Was she really a "two-bit Helen of Troy," as Earp expert Glenn Boyer described her?

Josephine Sarah Marcus was the daughter of middle-class, Jewish-German immigrants, a slim, pretty, dark-eyed girl with a strange accent. Details of her early life, including the year and place of her birth, have been clouded by her secrecy, although most historians agree she probably was born in Brooklyn, New York, in 1861.

Young Josie had a strong sense of adventure and a passion for the theatrical. In 1879, while living with her family in San Francisco, she and friend Dora Hirsch ran off to become dancers in actress Pauline Markham's traveling theater troupe. Josie didn't offer a word of explanation to her parents.

In an attempt to write her memoirs, written 50 years after the fact, she described herself and Dora as "two, giddy, stage-struck girls setting out in the world with very little equipment except their looks."

What captured their attention was the craze over *H.M.S. Pinafore*, a comic opera by Gilbert and Sullivan. The Markham troupe probably played Tombstone in December, 1879, then set out for Prescott. While en route, Josie met the charming, darkly handsome Behan, a Yavapai County deputy sheriff riding with a posse in pursuit of three stage robbers.

Johnny had a strong appetite for women, so it's easy to imagine him ignoring his sworn duty and departing the posse to escort the coach full of young actresses on to Prescott. His choice was Josie, who said later that her "heart was stirred by his attentions."

Shortly thereafter, when homesickness drove her back to her parents' home, Johnny came calling with a proposal. "He had thought of me ever since we had met," Josie explained. "He said he wanted me to become his wife. . . . I was not at all sure that I cared enough for him to marry him, and so he returned to Arizona."

But Behan was persistent, even sending someone to plead to his case. When Josie weighed the boredom of life with her parents in San Francisco against raucous Tombstone, she changed her mind. By the fall of 1880, she was — in her version — living with a town lawyer and his wife and keeping house for Behan and his 10-year-old son, Albert. The truth, more likely, was that 19-year-old Josie and 34-year-old Behan were living together.

The promised wedding, however, kept getting pushed back, and Johnny kept fooling around with other women. When Josie told her father of the situation, he sent $300 to pay for her return to San Francisco. Behan convinced her to use the money to help build a home for the two of them. Josie still believed his promise of marriage, and also pawned a diamond ring to help pay for the house construction.

But by the summer of 1881, Behan was caught in an adulterous affair, and Josie's affections switched permanently to Wyatt. The loss was painful and public for Behan. Author Casey Tefertiller, in his book *Wyatt Earp: The Life Behind the Legend*, wrote that this rejection was reported in the *Tombstone Epitaph* and that the humiliation was deep because she was considered Behan's wife, although no minister had married them.

Josie ultimately decided that Johnny was unscrupulous and money-grubbing, "a pompous little dandy." She offered those observations in *I Married Wyatt Earp*, a book combining Josie's recollections with Boyer's historical recreations.

Another story from that volume tells of Behan teaching Josie to ride a horse at Antelope Spring, southeast of Tombstone. When he spotted Apaches on a ridge, Behan said, "Pretend we haven't seen them and start for town slow. Don't act scared."

As the Indians gave chase, Behan shouted, "Run for it!" and sank his spurs into his horse. Josie's horse followed, although she had to struggle to hang on. Behan never looked back. "I could've been lying unconscious in the sagebrush from a tumble off the horse for all he knew," Josie said.

In Earp, she saw someone much different: "Wyatt was a man, a fact that made me see that Johnny had been something less."

The rift between the two men was only one cause of the Tombstone trouble. A stagecoach robbery and murder near Benson on March 15, 1881, was another, even hotter spark. In its aftermath, Behan, who had conspired with the stage robbers, allowed one of them to walk away from his jail. And he accused Wyatt's friend, Doc Holliday, of complicity in the Benson stage crime, undoubtedly as a means of discrediting Earp.

By October 26, 1881, the day of the O.K. Corral fight, the fuse had sizzled down to the powder. Josie was home that afternoon when she heard the shooting start.

"I knew in my heart it could be only one thing," she said in her recollections. "A picture flashed through my mind of Wyatt falling before the gunfire of Johnny's horrible poker-playing cronies. . . . Without stopping for a bonnet I rushed outside and toward the sound of the firing."

She begged a wagon ride to the scene of the gunfight and swooned when she spotted Wyatt, still standing. "My only thought was, 'My God, I haven't got a bonnet on. What will they think?' But you can imagine my relief at seeing my love alive. I was simply a little hysterical."

Josie's departure from Tombstone, early in 1882, marked the start of a remarkable odyssey. She and Wyatt spent the next 47 years living the vagabond life, hunting for gold in Idaho and Nevada, running race horses in San Diego and Oakland, and operating saloons in turn-of-the-century Alaskan boom camps. But the picture she painted of those years, full of romance and roses, was partly fiction.

In truth, their relationship was stormy and marred by tremendous fights. Josie was much like her husband — tough, hot-tempered, cantankerous in the extreme, though charming when it paid well.

Another shared trait, one that colored their lives together, was gambling. Much has been written about Wyatt's life as a professional gambler, a practice he was unable to control. But Josie was an addicted gambler as well.

Author Tefertiller tells of her getting money from millionaire friend Lucky Baldwin in return for a piece of jewelry, hoping to redeem it when her horse came in. But she rarely won, admitting that her bets were made "with more fresh-handedness than wisdom." Wyatt's patience with her wore thin as more and more of the jewelry he'd given her wound up in Baldwin's possession.

According to Tefertiller, Wyatt told his wife, "You have no business risking money that way. Now after this I'm not going to redeem any more of your jewelry."

But she rarely listened to her husband, or anyone else.

Stuart Lake, Wyatt's first biographer, learned of her difficult nature during his collaboration with the old marshal, beginning in 1928. When Wyatt died a year later in Los Angeles, with the book near completion, Josie's efforts to shape the manuscript became intolerable.

She feared what Lake knew and sought to protect her image and Wyatt's. When he arrived in Tombstone, Earp was married, at least by common law, to Mattie Blaylock, and he humiliated her in his dalliance with Josie. But Josie had an even more unflattering secret to keep — she had done a turn as a prostitute during her time in Tombstone. Lake, relying on information from Earp friend Bat Masterson, described Josie in a letter to his editor as "the belle of the honky-tonks, the prettiest dame in three hundred or so of her kind."

So eager was Josie to control the book project that she traveled to Boston in 1930 for a teary meeting with the publisher. She pulled the same power play nine years later when 20th Century Fox tried to film *Wyatt Earp: Frontier Marshal*, starring Randolph Scott. Boyer described her storming the studio with demands about how her husband's story should be told, so intimidating executives that production was halted. She got Wyatt's name removed from the picture, which was released simply as *Frontier Marshal*.

Josie's irrational behavior after Wyatt's death was probably intensified by grief. On the morning of January 19, 1929, when he breathed his last, Josie recalled in *I Married Wyatt Earp* that she held her husband's body in her arms, unable to let go. "They finally had to drag me away," she said.

She was too distraught to attend Wyatt's funeral and even kept his cremated remains in her home for six months, according to California writer Susan Silva. Finally, in July, she boarded a train for Hills of Eternity Cemetery outside San Francisco, carrying the ashes in a common urn wrapped in a towel, the whole package stuffed into a satchel. In her memoirs, she wrote that she must've looked "like some queer old granny" as she sought to give her man a proper burial.

In her last years, in Los Angeles, Josie must've spent many an hour remembering her days as a pretty, prancing teenager who helped put Tombstone on the map and keep it there. But she also suffered from frequent bouts of depression, nagging health problems, and loneliness, although she did maintain a lifelong correspondence with Albert Behan, the boy she'd cared for so long before.

But no matter where she went, or what she did, Josie was forever associated with Wyatt, either tainted or sainted by his name. Because she was Mrs. Earp, she was invited to dine in Hollywood with such luminaries as Cecil B. DeMille and Gary Cooper, and she was sought out for her opinions on frontier life. She received money from Lake's book and the Fox production, but it was hardly enough, particularly for an addicted gambler, and she was perpetually broke.

"Toward the end, she survived by getting handouts from anyone she could," says Long Beach, California, writer Lee Silva, whose first volume of *Wyatt Earp: A Biography of the Legend*, was published in 1998. "One of those who helped her was William S. Hart, the movie actor. I found one of his canceled checks to Josie for $100, and I assume he loaned her money other times, too."

When Josie died on December 20, 1944, at 84, her funeral drew a handful of people. Of the hundreds who attended Wyatt's service, including wealthy businessmen and movie celebrities, only Hart came to Josie's.

"That's a particularly poignant image to me," says Silva. "A friend had to pay for her funeral, and only Hart showed up to say good-bye." Josie is buried beside Wyatt at the Hills of Eternity cemetery, in Colma.

CHAPTER SIX

Ida Genung

Stories told by her family relate how legendary mountain man Paulino Weaver taught young Ida masculine skills, including roping, swearing, and chewing tobacco. At age 22, she moved with her husband and baby son to a ranch in Peeples Valley, where they lived 12 miles from the nearest neighbor in an area with hostile Indians on the prowl.

⊰——⊱

VEN AT AGE 22, IDA GENUNG HAD STEEL IN HER SPINE. So when she came upon a badly shot-up man, lying on canvas on the dirt floor of a prospector's cabin, his head resting on a stick of wood, she never hesitated.

"Charley," she said to her husband, "get me some clean clothes and a pillow for his head."

Then she dropped to her knees and went to work on his wounds, putting aside the thoughts that must have flooded her mind.

Barely four months before, she had given birth to her first son in the safety of her parents' home in San Bernardino, California. Now she was back in Arizona's Yavapai County, and the homecoming wasn't quite what she had expected. She must have wondered what would become of baby Frank in this wild place. Might the Indians do to him what they had done to John Burger, the settler at her feet?

Burger was on his way to get supplies when his mule saw the Indians and bucked him off. The warriors grabbed his rifle and began firing. With a bullet wound in his thigh, Burger scrambled behind some boulders. But as the Indians kept shooting, the slugs broke apart on the big rocks, sending lead splinters into his body.

"He looked as though he was shot to pieces," Ida recalled years later. "I washed him, and it took me over two hours to soak the blood out of his ears and hair alone."

An Army doctor was on his way from Camp Date Creek. Ida wanted to make Burger comfortable, so she and Charley cleaned and dressed him before they said good-bye. They never expected to see him alive again.

The Genungs were headed for their ranch in Peeples Valley. It was the spring of 1871, and the chances of a white couple surviving, 12 miles from the nearest neighbor with hostile Indians on the prowl, were not good. But Ida, a blunt-spoken woman who wouldn't be sassed, even by the toughest cowboy, had hitched her fate to the frontier, and to Charley.

She first came to the Arizona Territory in March, 1869, at age 20. She was born in Council Bluffs, Iowa, the daughter of army doctor Isaac Smith, who moved his family west in 1852. On their arrival in California, the Smiths met Paulino Weaver, the trapper and explorer, who already was well known in Arizona. Weaver was bedridden with rheumatism, but under Dr. Smith's care, he recovered. He showed his thanks by giving the Smiths a parcel of his land in the San Bernardino Mountains.

Smith family tradition states that Weaver taught young Ida to rope, swear, and chew tobacco, the latter two habits drawing her mother's strong disapproval. "She could ride a horse or drive a freight team better than most of the men," wrote Prescott historian Sharlot Hall in 1931, "and she had a trick of throwing the loop of a riata [lariat] around the nose of a wild horse as none of them could ever learn to do."

New York-born Charley Genung, who moved to San Francisco with his mother when he was 11, probably met blonde, blue-eyed Ida in 1863. Charley began working the placer finds of Rich Hill in Yavapai County that year. He was back in California in 1868 on a horse-buying expedition. But even in his memoirs, Charley provided few details of his courtship of

**IDA GENUNG SURVIVED FLOODS, APACHES,
AND FIRES TO LIVE TO A RIPE OLD AGE.**

Ida, except to say, "I have a sweetheart in California." They were married February 16, 1869.

Ida's wedding gifts from her parents included a milk cow named Mott and a team of mules. She drove them into Arizona the next month for what Charley promised was a one-year stay. Ida was forced to handle the reins herself after one of the mules kicked Charley, injuring his leg.

"I'll have to use all the swear words Paulino Weaver taught me to get these cussed beasts to Arizona," Ida said.

They crossed the Colorado River on a ferry pulled by an Indian riding a horse, a rope tied to his saddle horn. Ida asked that her mules and Mott be unhitched from the wagon, drawing guffaws from onlookers. "If anything happens," she insisted, "I want them to be able to swim so I can grab the reins and get hauled to shore." They made it across safely. As Ida re-tied Mott to the wagon, she heard frantic screams. She and

Charley turned to see the Indian and his horse founder and drown in the rushing water.

The Genungs moved on to Montgomery mine, on the Hassayampa River, where they were met by six friends. Using a makeshift stove set up under a tree, Ida cooked a meal, including six dried-apple pies, but they didn't get to enjoy it. Mott ate it all while she wasn't looking. Ida prepared a cornmeal mush, the only food she had left. The men choked it down and graciously declared it "the best meal they'd had in months."

Ida panned for gold, pulling enough from the river to buy boots for Charley. But within weeks, Apache raiders drove them away. "I concluded that the locality was too dangerous a place in which to keep a brand-new wife," Charley wrote in a letter to Ida's parents.

The Genungs went to nearby Walnut Grove, but they didn't remain there long either. Margaret Maxwell, writing in the *Journal of Arizona History* in 1984, said that Charley, unable to pay $1,300 he owed another rancher, agreed to settle with a game of seven-up. If he won, the debt was retired; if not, he would lose his spread.

The cards turned against Charley, and he and Ida moved again, settling in Peeples Valley in March, 1870. "The Indians had driven out all the settlers up to this time," Charley said. "However, my bad luck had made me properly hostile, and I determined to take a chance at it."

In a letter to her parents, Ida described the valley: "Wire grass as high as a man's knees on horseback, a stream of clear sparkling water; flowers, violets, buttercups, sego lilies — you should see them. . . . The woods are mostly walnut trees; under them are stacks of metate stones used by the Indians to crack nuts and grind corn. We hear quail constantly, and see lots of ducks and wild deer."

She also dropped the news that she was pregnant. Ida told Charley that she would rather have the baby at her parents' home, which she did on January 13, 1871. While returning to Arizona with infant Frank, she and Charley came upon Burger in that cabin near Rich Hill. To their surprise, he survived, thanks to Ida's care, and spent a year recuperating at the Genung ranch.

But even there, fear was part of Ida's life. Rather than remain at the ranch alone while Charley was off mining or road-building, she frequently stayed with neighbors. In the summer of 1871, Charley took her to the Bowers' Ranch in Skull Valley to await his return from a two-night trip. As he departed, Ida reminded him, "Don't forget the indigo!"

While in Prescott, Charley joined a posse to chase renegades who had taken part in a deadly raid. After 19 days, during which the posse killed 56 Apaches and recovered 133 stolen horses, Charley returned to Skull Valley, handed Ida his holsters, with indigo stuffed inside, and said: "Here's the indigo, wife, and I had a helluva time getting it."

Ida knew something about guns herself. She never ventured far from her two Colt .45 pistols, even when doing housework. Maxwell wrote that they were given to her, along with a mastiff named Pete, by her brother.

Once baby Frank became ill while Judge Frank Kelsey, of Kirkland, was visiting the Genungs. He suggested that his wife, who had a knack for doctoring, treat the child. Ida and Kelsey jumped into a buggy, with the baby wedged between them and a Colt pistol at Ida's feet. In his biography of Charley Genung, *Death in His Saddlebags*, California author Dan Genung, Charley and Ida's grandson, wrote that hostiles appeared on a ridge top and raced to cut off the travelers. Ida whipped her team to a gallop.

Kelsey shouted, "Give me the gun!"

"I give my gun to no one!" she replied and beat the riders to Kirkland.

Indians even lurked in the tall grass around Ida's backyard garden. Helen Chapman Wilburn, her granddaughter, said that before going outside, Ida would send Pete to sniff out trouble. If the dog returned wagging his tail, Ida knew it was safe; if the hair on his back was standing, she stayed indoors.

"After a while, Gram realized the Indians didn't want to kill her," said Wilburn. "They had plenty of chance to do that. They were just curious."

Ida's garden became something of a landmark. Settlers rarely passed through Peeples Valley without tasting her fruits and vegetables. Such luxuries were rare until Ida brought the seeds into the territory. She shared her expertise with many others, helping gardens spring up across the county.

Word of her generosity made the Genung ranch a way-station for travelers, overnight guests, even wandering Indians. Ida befriended many of the Indians and learned their methods of healing. She knew how to use squawberry and tea to treat stomach ailments and how to ease a head cold by burning tarbush and sniffing the smoke.

One of her close friends, a Yavapai woman, became part of the Genung family after Charley saved her life. He was building a road between Congress and Peeples Valley when an Indian girl ran toward him, fleeing a Tonto brave trying to burn her as a witch. Charley drove him off with his rifle and brought the girl to the ranch. Indian Mary formed a bond with Ida that lasted until the end of her life. She called Ida "Mama."

Ida had eight children of her own. Her fourth, Mabel Amanda, was born at the ranch in 1875. The delivery left Ida with a prolapsed uterus, requiring surgery. She packed her four kids into a coach for a grueling, three-hour ride to the nearest railhead, then took the train to Los Angeles. When Mabel became a doctor in 1911, she received her degree from the same physician who had operated on Ida.

Even after the Indian threat had passed, frontier life remained dangerous. Three times from 1878 to 1889, the Genung house burned to the ground. Charley, an occasional lawman, was certain that two of those blazes were set by outlaws seeking revenge.

In the winter of 1890, Ida narrowly escaped death in a massive flood along the Hassayampa River. She was traveling to Phoenix, amid heavy rains, with six-year-old daughter, Grace, and hired hand Mike Boland. In Dan Genung's account, they forded the flooded river at the Seymour stage stop and prepared to spend the night. Then Ida had a premonition.

"Mike, I don't like the looks of things," she said. "Hitch up again and let's get moving."

They were barely out of the river basin when a 40-foot wall of water obliterated everything in its path. "If I live to be a thousand years," Grace said, "I'll never forget my mother's scream."

Charley died of Bright's disease in 1916. Ida lived another 17 years and was rarely lonely. When her sons were off rounding up cattle, Indian Mary, fretting that her good friend would be unattended, came to stay. She would drop a pallet on the floor beside Ida's bed and sleep there until the boys came home.

On her 83rd birthday in 1931, two years before her death, the woman known throughout Yavapai County as Gram was feted at the old governor's mansion in Prescott, her children and grandchildren by her side. It's tempting to wonder if, on that fine night, Ida thought back to the day she saved Burger's life and to what had happened in the ensuing 61 years. If so, she surely smiled with satisfaction at the state she helped build.

Pearl Hart

*She eloped at age 16, suffered physical abuse
from her husband, bounced around the West
with two children, and ended up broke
when the boarding house where she worked
closed. Then, in 1899, after she and a
half-wit partner robbed one of the West's
last stage coaches, she declared: "I shall not
consent to be tried under a law in which
my sex had no voice in making," and she
became a cause célèbre.*

———◆———

P EARL HART DEPARTED THIS REALM LATE ON THE AFTER-
noon of May 30, 1899, when she leveled her .36-cal-
iber pistol at three stagecoach passengers outside
Globe. From that moment on, the homely, marijuana-smoking
saloon singer was transformed into a gorgeous fantasy, a 5-
foot-tall, 100-pound dream in a grubby range hat.

She became a creation of writers seeking a good story
and of her own frustrated dreams. After her arrest, when reporters came poking around, the Canadian-born, 28-year-old
lit up brighter than a bordello on Saturday night, tossing out
rich quotes to *Cosmopolitan* magazine and posing with guns
for New York photographers. She wasn't especially expert at
using them, of course, but by then everyone was winking to
the same lie.

What Pearl Hart really was, and how she was portrayed,
weren't at all the same. In the gap between real woman and lady
bandit, between blood and ink, stands a story about a territory

**HAIR SHORN AND WEARING PRISON STRIPES,
PEARL WAS PHOTOGRAPHED LOOKING LESS THAN HAPPY.**

and a nation that had no idea how to deal with a rebellious, troubled, intelligent, talented female, prone to fabulously bad choices in men.

Pearl Taylor was born in Lindsay, Ontario, in 1871. As a 16-year-old boarding school student, she eloped with a man who physically abused her. This first attempt at a relationship with Hart was short-lived, and she and her baby soon returned to her mother's side. But when Hart summoned her back, she obeyed and the beatings continued.

"After bearing up under his blows as long as I could," Pearl told *Cosmopolitan* in October, 1899, "I left him again."

She made her way to Chicago in 1893 and saw Annie Oakley shoot playing cards from her husband's hand at Buffalo Bill's West Show. She also visited the women's pavilion at the World's Fair to listen to speeches by well-known suffragettes, such as Julia Ward Howe.

"Something happened to Pearl there," says Jane Candia

Coleman, author of a novel about Pearl's life. "She saw women getting out and doing things, and this impressed her. But she was still married to this bum, and I think she thought a lot about that."

When the fair closed, Pearl hopped a train to Trinidad, Colorado, and made a living singing for tips in saloons. But the press, eager to doll up her story, later reported that she sold herself as a prostitute. Pearl contributed to that falsehood by telling *Cosmopolitan* that she was "21, good-looking, and ready for anything that might come."

After Trinidad, and several other towns, she landed in Phoenix and came face to face on the street with her husband. Again she described herself in ways that made speculation of prostitution inevitable: "I was not the innocent schoolgirl he had enticed from home. . . . I had been inured to the hardships of the world and knew much of its wickedness."

For unexplained reasons, Pearl felt the old infatuation and spent another three years with him, bearing a second child. But his beatings didn't stop, and she left him for good. She shipped her kids back to her mother, then living in Ohio, and eventually made her way to Globe, where she worked in a miner's boarding house alongside a half-wit named Joe Boot.

He was another man with absolutely nothing going for him, except an ability to talk a vulnerable young woman into a stagecoach heist that had no chance of succeeding. But Pearl had to try, because her mom, "my dearest, truest friend," was sick. With the boarding house closed down, and the mining claims she and Boot worked yielding nothing but blisters, she was desperate for money to hurry to her mother's bedside.

The robbery of one of the West's last stagecoaches was done largely on impulse. It yielded some $430 and a .45-caliber revolver that Pearl took from driver Henry Bacon. But the newspaper copy that came from it was worth a million bucks.

Within days of landing in the Florence jail, the Territory was caught in a Pearl Hart frenzy.

"Arizona rejoiced in the possession of a female bandit,"

PEARL HART IN A TOUGH POSE.

wrote state historian James McClintock in 1916 about the jour-
nalistic jamboree that followed.

The press portrayed Pearl as a desperado with a full
bosom, clad in overalls and a man's shirt. Reporters delighted
in recalling the orders she barked to the stunned passengers.

"Get out and line up!" Pearl had shouted, showing her
gun. "Get out, quick!"

After she shook down the three men for their booty, she
swaggered up and down before them with the traditional cold
eye and twisted lip, one reporter wrote. Then she peeled three

singles from a roll of stolen bills and gave one to each man.

"For grub and lodging," she said. "Now climb aboard and don't look back for 10 minutes!"

The better and truer angle, one that wouldn't play in the turn-of-the-century West, was her understandable contempt for men.

It flared five days after the robbery when Sheriff William Truman's posse surprised the sleeping outlaws 20 miles outside Benson. Pearl jumped to her feet and lashed into Boot, her lover, for not resisting, showing what Truman called the nerve of a tiger cat. "She would've killed me if she could," he said.

Later, in describing to *Cosmopolitan* the ease with which the passengers gave up their guns, Pearl made a crack about the cowardice of men that carried a distinctly feminist tone: "Really, I can't see why men carry revolvers, because they almost invariably give them up at the very time they were made to be used."

The best twist, however, was Pearl becoming an advocate for women's suffrage. From her cell, she wrote a letter to the prosecuting attorney that echoed with the semi-awakening she experienced at the World's Fair. "I shall not consent to be tried under a law in which my sex had no voice in making," she wrote.

For someone whose life was on the line, the declaration was a brilliant appeal to public opinion, and a sentiment she undoubtedly endorsed. After her October 11, 1899, escape from the jail in Tucson, where she'd been transferred, that city's powerful newspaper took up her cause.

"Pearl Hart . . . raised a most important question, which shows the injustice which is visited upon her sex," wrote the *Arizona Daily Star*. "To carry out what she deemed her right under the principles of our government, she struck out for liberty."

If the Territory's citizens were upset at Pearl's seeming inability to obey anyone's law, the *Star* didn't let on. In one of the most tortured arguments heard in the entire matter, the paper attempted to explain the popularity of this rogue outlaw by citing, of all things, chivalry.

"Every true frontiersman hallows the thought that his mother was a woman," the paper mused, "and he owes respect and protection to her sex, no matter where she may be, nor what her misfortunes might have been."

Pearl's misfortunes, all of her own making, continued after the escape. She and her getaway partner — Ed Logan, a drunk and the champion bicycle thief of Phoenix — were captured in Deming, New Mexico, by lawman George Scarborough. She was wearing men's clothes, but he recognized her from a photo published in *Cosmopolitan*, and Scarborough later told newsmen she had "the foulest mouth he'd ever seen."

By that time, Pearl was surely playing to her public. "She had a marvelous time showing off to reporters," said Coleman, author of *I, Pearl Hart*, published in 1998 by Five Star Western books. "She was a singer, remember, who had a captive audience, and she rode it for all it was worth."

At the trial, held in Florence in November, 1899, Boot pleaded guilty to stage robbery and was given 30 years. Pearl, adopting yet another persona, wept before the jury and won acquittal by claiming that her desire to see her mother had made her "temporarily insane."

But Judge Fletcher Doan angrily lectured the jurors on their decision. He ordered Pearl to stand trial again, this time for stealing Bacon's gun. After 30 minutes of deliberation, she was found guilty and ordered to spend the next five years at Yuma.

Pearl's celebrity didn't diminish with her conviction. On the train ride to the pen, she reverted to her desperado pose, puffing on cigars that rivaled "the effect of the locomotive to charge the atmosphere with smoke." And within a few weeks of her arriving in the Colorado River town, the *Yuma Sun* was reporting that Pearl was "a morphine fiend of the most depraved character and at present is rather hard to get along with."

By January of 1900, the publicity had finally brought Paul

**STILL BOYISHLY DRESSED AS AN INMATE,
PEARL IS PETTING A CAT WHILE SHE READS.**

Hull, editor of *Arizona Graphic* magazine, to the limits of his patience. What sent him over the edge was a story in the *New York Journal* stating that Pearl had broken jail at Tucson, was still at liberty, and a terror to every law officer of the Southwest — published three months after she'd been caught, tried, and sent to prison.

"I would respectfully ask of the yellow journals," Hull wrote, "that they give us a rest on Pearl Hart, and take up their old favorites, 'Alkali Ike,' 'Rattlesnake Pete,' and other society leaders of this land of tarantulas and bug juice."

The trouble with defining Pearl is that she couldn't define herself. She told a lot of different stories, lied when it was necessary to cover her tracks, and seemed caught in a never-ending process of inventing herself. Writers were left to grab for easy stereotypes, such the *Daily Star's* statement that her "countenance does not bear the stamp of any great intelligence."

But as part of her research, author Coleman tracked down surviving family members and had access to the diary Pearl kept in later years. She wrote in what Coleman called a "beautiful hand" and expressed her thoughts in "quite a literate way."

How much better would her story have been if the cartoon image of the dull-eyed and brutish road agent was dropped for the complex truth: A sharp young woman, on her own, trapped by foul circumstance and an addiction to laudanum, driving herself to a bad fate, in part due to a powerful itch for men.

In 1954, many years after the newspapers had forgotten her name, the Arizona Historical Society received a letter from a man who claimed to be an acquaintance of Pearl's when she was a teenager in Peterborough, Canada. In his letter, William B. Davey said that she was widely admired, but had a single fault that brought her many troubles.

"She accepted too many dates with handsome young men, which finally caused her undoing," wrote the Joplin, Missouri, resident. "She was too amorous."

But throughout her life, Pearl made her own choices, including orchestrating her resurrection. She accomplished it by pulling off one of the West's great disappearing acts. After gaining early release from Yuma in 1902, she was last heard from two years later when newspapers in Kansas City reported that she was busted for her role in a pickpocket ring.

From then on, nothing. Pearl Hart and all her guises dropped from public view.

She spent the final 50 years of her life as a rancher's wife in Dripping Springs, Arizona, not far from the scene of the robbery. She went by the name Pearl Bywater.

Globe writer Clara Woody was the first to reveal her true identity. She pieced together the mystery of the dark-eyed Mrs.

Bywater while visiting the ranch as a census taker in 1940. Woody said the room in which Mrs. Bywater lived was littered with cigar butts, its resident sloppily dressed.

It was Pearl all right, living happily, tending a garden, scribbling in her diary, and revealing only to her husband who she really was.

"She was shy, retiring and talked to nobody," says Coleman. "At that stage of her life, I believe she wanted to disappear, and did. She'd lived a heckuva life and deserved a little peace."

Pearl Hart Bywater died in 1956, at 85, still doing what she wanted to do, after all those years.

CHAPTER EIGHT

Josephine Brawley Hughes

*She held a baby in her arms and kept a rifle
at her side during a five-day coach trip in 1872
across the desert from San Diego, California,
to Tucson, Arizona. She immediately set herself
to tasks to "civilize" the region, first by
introducing candles to Tucson and eventually
by waging war against liquor and saloons
and fighting for women's suffrage.*

THROUGHOUT HER LIFE, JOSEPHINE BRAWLEY HUGHES
sought to please only her conscience. Such a taskmaster
it was, too, puritan in its disapproval of whiskey and saloons, radical in its demand for women's suffrage. For both
causes, and many others, she worked ceaselessly, without a
thought of personal popularity. A good thing, too, because at
times in her life she was widely disliked.

Animosity followed Josephine. She was stern and single-
minded, a moral scold whose certainty of mission left little
room for human weakness. Those traits show in her photographs — thin lips, lantern jaw, hard and disapproving eyes.
She was not to be trifled with.

E. Josephine Brawley, daughter of farmer and lawyer John R.
Brawley, was born on a farm near Meadville, Pennsylvania, on December 22, 1839. Evidently she disliked her first name, Elizabeth,
and dropped it later in life. According to various accounts, she
attended a small school 70 miles from home, then graduated
from Edinboro State Normal School and taught for two years.

While at Edinboro, she met Louis C. Hughes, a law student working in her father's office. They married in 1868. Trouble caused by a Civil War wound prompted Louis to move to Tucson, Arizona Territory, in 1871, joining his older brother, Sam. Louis opened a law office and within a year had saved enough money for Josephine to join him. She traveled with her baby daughter, Gertrude, by rail to San Francisco and by steamboat to San Diego. From there, it was across the desert to Tucson, a 400-mile journey of difficulty and danger.

For five days and nights — the coach stopping only to change horses — Josephine bounced over mountains and across the desert. She held Gertrude in her arms, wrapped in a linen duster, and kept a loaded rifle by her side. The coach traveled at high speed over terrible roads, causing Josephine to fear that her rifle might discharge.

At one point, the horses stumbled and the coach lurched, sending Gertrude into the air and onto soft sand below. Josephine ordered the team to a halt and jumped down to collect her little daughter. She climbed back aboard, and with a whip and a holler, the coach was off again. Gertrude was unhurt in the incident.

Various newspaper stories state that Josephine's arrival made her the third white woman to settle in Tucson. The number might not be far off. In 1872, the tiny village on the Santa Cruz River was predominantly Mexican and still primitive. But Josephine would see to it that change was fast in coming.

In a profile published in the *Arizona Historical Review* in January, 1930, author C. Louise Boehringer described how Josephine went about "civilizing" her new home. When she saw that night-time light was provided by rags floating in a saucer of grease, she sent back to Pennsylvania for candle molds. Soon Josephine's home, and those of her neighbors, were lighted by candles.

She believed the water delivered to homes by wagons, and sold by peddlers at 10 cents a bucket, was unsanitary, so she ordered the construction of a cistern, possibly the first in Arizona. She also had the first board floor in a Tucson home, the first grass lawn, and the first parlor carpet — purchased at the exorbitant cost of $240. It was shipped from San Francisco to Yuma, ferried across the Colorado River, and hauled over the desert by wagon train.

"The carpet came in strips that were sewed together by hand and laid upon layers of straw and paper," Boehringer wrote. "The whole family sat upon it and stretched and pulled until it was tacked in place."

In addition to Gertrude, the family included a son John, born in 1874, and a daughter, Josephine, born three years later. Another daughter died as a toddler and was laid to rest in the front yard of the Hughes home, with a rose bush at each end of the plot. Burying her in the town cemetery was out of the question for Josephine because it was overrun with coyotes.

Louis' law practice, and his success in a string of political jobs, helped place the Hughes family among Tucson's most powerful. Their home became a kind of headquarters for prominent women and men from around the Territory. Gen. Nelson Miles visited in 1886. He headed the government's campaign against the Apaches and used the Hughes' dining room table to spread out his war maps and plot strategy.

Josephine entered public life through the schoolhouse door. In 1873, after his appointment as county superintendent of schools, Louis authorized the founding of Tucson's first public school for girls. He hired two female teachers from California, but Apaches made it too dangerous for them to travel to southern Arizona. Josephine filled the void by starting the school herself, hoping it would add to the "moral tone" of the community, and served briefly as its first teacher.

She also was instrumental in founding Tucson's Congregational Church, which was the first Protestant Church in the Territory, although her motivation wasn't entirely pure. She strongly disliked Roman Catholicism and sought to counter its dominance in Tucson. As soon as the building was complete, Josephine switched allegiance to the Methodists, and helped raised money to build a church for them.

JOSEPHINE BRAWLEY HUGHES IN HER LATER YEARS.

The imposing brick edifice opened in Tucson in 1881, and over the next two decades became a rallying place for several reform movements. At Josephine's request, Frances W. Willard, a Hughes friend and leader of the Women's Christian Temperance Union (WCTU), spoke at the Methodist church in March of 1883. The result was the founding of a local WCTU chapter, with Josephine as president. The two women toured the Territory to set up chapters, drawing like-minded women and men to rousing meetings at which they issued sobriety oaths and pinned white ribbons on converts.

"Oh, Christian women! Oh, friends of the Territory!" boomed Josephine in one speech. "Do you not feel your responsibilities!?

. . . The dreaded Apache has slain his hundreds. Strong drink has slain its thousands."

The temperance union in 1884 persuaded the legislature to forbid the sale of whiskey on election days and to make it illegal for boys under 16 to enter saloons. The sale of liquor on Sundays was outlawed a few years later. Josephine's work laid the groundwork for prohibition, which became Arizona law on January 1, 1915, four years before booze was banned nationally.

The victory was judged remarkable in a state that many saw as the heart of the "wet West." But to saloon men and occasional tipplers, Josephine and her ilk were part of "that damned white-ribboned scourge."

Energy and intellect played a big role in Josephine's success. But so did her husband's power — he was appointed governor in 1893 — and his ownership of *The Arizona Daily Star*, the Territory's first daily newspaper. Louis and Josephine both believed that it was right and proper to use the paper to promote their causes. Although her titles were bookkeeper, business manager, and cashier, Josephine's hand is all through its pages. Her ideals became the *Star's*.

The paper was righteously Democratic and pro woman. It also was opposed to capital punishment, gambling, even the curse of high skirts. In one story, Josephine reported on a woman reformer who appeared in Chicago wearing a dress with a hem 18 inches off the ground. She wrote such might be necessary in a dirty city like Chicago, but never in Arizona.

On drinking, the *Star* was unrelenting. Even though their policy caused a near revolt among employees, the Hughes' insisted on paying workers early in the week, rather than on Saturdays. The latter gave the men money for a weekend binge, making it harder to publish the Monday edition. The *Star* also refused to take advertising from any business that profited from the sale of liquor, a costly stand at a time when much of a newspaper's revenue came from saloons.

R.A. Carples, who once ran the paper while Louis was

traveling in the east, was unaware of the prohibition and published a saloon ad.

"The first paper she [Josephine] saw, she came down and gave me the devil," said Carples, in a bulletin published by the University Press in 1950. "When L.C. [Louis] came home, she climbed him. When he asked her for a copy, she said she'd burned every one soon as it came into the house."

The Hughes' dislike of whiskey was occasionally insidious. With Josephine egging him on, Louis used his clout to hector public officials who enjoyed a boost now and again. Col. J. Hampton Hoge met their wrath when Hughes, in 1893, forced him out of his job with the U.S. Consular Service after he was seen drunk on a train. The action earned Louis bitter political enemies.

The paper's opinions on the Apache question were harsh as well. "Let our motto be removal or extermination," thundered one editorial, published in 1883. "Civilization demands it. Self-protection will enforce it."

But on women's suffrage, the *Star's* words rang with elegance: "We have pioneer women in Arizona who for a quarter of a century have given their best life to the building of schools, churches and social institutions for the benefit of this territory — who came to Arizona in the pride of useful womanhood and who are now wearing the snow-white locks. They ask for justice and fair dealing, and . . . privileges of citizenship, irrespective of sex."

The suffrage fight was Josephine's finest hour. As she had done with Willard in 1883, she summoned to Arizona a prominent figure in the national movement. Laura M. Johns, of Kansas, came to the Territory in 1891 and helped form the Arizona Suffrage Association. Within three years, the cause so consumed Josephine that she resigned as head of the local WCTU.

"Let us secure the vote for women first," she said, "then the victory for the protection of our homes and for the cause of temperance will follow."

Several times in the 1890s, calls for women's suffrage were heard in the Territorial legislature, but they were defeated each time. Victory came, oddly enough, after Josephine's son, John, a senator in the state's first legislature, took up the cause. It was an issue he was bred to fight. At the national suffrage convention in 1890, leader Susan B. Anthony, a friend of Josephine's, grabbed young John, then 16, and brought him to the rostrum before thousands of women.

In recounting the incident in 1939, John Murdock, an Arizona congressman, wrote that Anthony "laid hands upon his head with almost religious ceremony, and dubbed him the suffrage knight of Arizona." Because of John Hughes' efforts, and certainly those of his mother before him, a measure giving the vote to Arizona women was passed in November, 1912, seven years before national suffrage.

Josephine's influence began to wane after Louis was forced to resign as governor amid a fierce political dispute and charges of corruption. The family's power further diminished when Louis sold the *Star* in 1907, after 30 years of ownership. He died of pneumonia eight years later. In 1921, John Hughes, Josephine's beloved son, also died, a blow that stole much of her once indomitable spirit.

In 1925, while living with Gertrude in Hermosa Beach, California, Josephine broke her leg in a fall. The accident left her crippled and weak, and she died in March of the following year, at 88. In tributes given at her memorial service, she was called the Mother of Arizona and praised in a way that often eluded her in life. A bronze tablet in her memory still adorns the rotunda of the state capitol building in Phoenix.

CHAPTER NINE

Emma Lee French

*An emigrant from Victorian England, she had
all the grit necessary for survival as a pioneer
in the American West. "I had no one to . . . look
out for me, so I decided that I must look out
for myself," she said later of a 1,400-mile trek
in which she pulled a handcart. Yet, she left
her deepest mark as one who cared for the
injured and sick in an untamed land.*

⟞⟩⟨⟝

T HE MOST STRIKING ASPECT OF EMMA BATCHELOR LEE
French's life was how unlikely it was. Consider a well-
educated woman, living in Uchfield, England, falling
under the sway of Mormon missionaries and deciding to leave
everything and follow them to Zion. Emma did this at 21. Not
in her deepest dreams could she have imagined becoming the
wife of an infamous Mormon killer, or the operator of a ferry
across the Colorado River, or a frontier doctor ministering to the
sick when no other help was available.

The magnitude of what she experienced, her triumphs
and tragedies, brings her story close to the realm of epic. So
does her courage. Standing 5 feet 6 inches tall, she was tough,
stout, occasionally hot-tempered, and spoke with a working-
class English accent.

Emma needed all of her grit to survive the trek across the
American continent. With passage paid by the Mormon Church,
she departed Liverpool on May 25, 1857, and sailed for the United
States. From the East Coast, she rode the rails to Iowa City, then
loaded her belongings onto a church-issued handcart and walked
1,400 miles to Salt Lake City, pulling her cart the entire way.

About 150 members of Emma's party died in vicious mountain snowstorms. The ground was frozen so hard that tent pegs couldn't be secured and the dead couldn't be buried. Many survivors suffered frozen feet, noses, and fingers. Along the way, Emma served as midwife to a pregnant woman, and for two days, according to her biographer, Juanita Brooks, she pulled the cart with the recovering mother inside.

"I had no one to . . . look out for me, so I decided that I must look out for myself," Emma said later, in describing her days as a handcart pioneer. "When we came to a stream, I stopped and took off my shoes and stockings and outer skirt and put them on top of the cart. Then, after I got the cart across, I came back and carried [a little boy] over on my back. Then I sat down and scrubbed my feet hard with my woolen handkerchief and put on dry shoes and stockings."

Shortly after arriving in Salt Lake, she met John Doyle Lee, a prominent Mormon colonist. The two were sealed in marriage by Brigham Young on January 7, 1858. She was Lee's 17th wife. In his diary, he wrote of Emma: "She covenanted to follow me through poverty, privation, or affliction to the end of her days and I believe that her intentions [are] real and integrity true."

Over the next 20 years, those words proved prophetic as Lee was hunted by federal marshals for his role in one of the frontier's most infamous incidents. At Mountain Meadows, Utah, 140 California-bound immigrants were butchered by Indians and Mormon militiamen. Lee was said to have led the attackers in the five-day slaughter.

In *Emma Lee*, her 1975 biography, Brooks wrote that Emma probably knew nothing about Lee's role in the massacre when she married him, four months later. But it haunted their lives together and marked them as outcasts, especially among other churchmen. In 1868, while living in Harmony, Utah, Lee received a letter warning him to leave the Mormon settlement within 10 days or face hanging.

Emma, ever loyal, confronted George Hicks, one of the

AFTER LIFE AT LONELY DELL, EMMA LEE FRENCH BECAME
WINSLOW'S UNOFFICIAL PHYSICIAN.

men she suspected of writing the threats, and warned him, according to Lee's diary, to "sing low and keep out of her path or she would put a load of buckshot in his backside."

Hicks complained to the bishop about Emma's unchristian behavior and a court was convened. The bishop decided she and Hicks should be re-baptized. Emma agreed, but asked the bishop do the baptizing, "seeing that you are so inconsiderate as to require a woman to be immersed when the water is full of snow and ice and that too for defending the rights of her husband."

Then she cranked up her sarcasm: "Perhaps if your backside gets wet in ice water you will be more careful how you decide again." The bishop let the matter drop.

JOHN LEE, EMMA'S FIRST HUSBAND.

The federal government didn't waver in its insistence that someone be brought to justice for Mountain Meadows. In response to the pressure, the Mormon Church in 1870 excommunicated Lee, but continued to assigned him to important tasks. Late in 1871, he was asked to establish a ferry crossing on the Colorado River, near the Arizona-Utah border, the only spot between Moab and Needles narrow enough for wagons to cross.

Lonely Dell, as Emma and John named it, was a beautiful place, framed by pink cliffs. For a time they were happy, building a fine home, a stone corral, a willow chicken coop, and clearing land to grow vegetables and alfalfa.

They greeted explorers and settlers who stopped for rest and re-supply. Among them was Maj. John Wesley Powell, the first man to explore the Colorado River through the Grand

Canyon. In August, 1872, on his second exploration of canyon country, the major and his party dined at the ferry and stayed the night. Also that summer, according to Brooks, the Powell group's photographer became ill with what was believed to be consumption. The ailing man, James Fennemore, was brought to Lonely Dell and left under Emma's care.

The best description of Emma's home at Lonely Dell, near today's Lees Ferry, comes from trader Don Maguire, who made several treks across northern Arizona in the 1870s. In his autobiography, published in *Utah Historical Quarterly* in 1985, he described the Lee home as a one-story log structure with six rooms. In one corner of the sitting room were six shotguns, a smooth-bore U.S. musket, and a brass-mounted Fremont rifle. Three Colt pistols hung on the walls. In other places, the walls were papered over with copies of the *New York Sun* and the *New York Tribune*.

Maguire wrote that Emma Lee was "a cross between a blond and a brunette . . . with small hands and feet, pleasing manners, rather inclined to smile than to be solemn."

But her life at Lonely Dell often was hard and dangerous. Lee was gone for long periods, tending to his other homes and wives, or evading the law. Emma had to manage the ferry and homestead herself, care for the children, and deal with occasional visits from Indians.

In August, 1873, a band of Navajos crossed the river and camped near the Lees' corral. They acted suspiciously, raising Emma's fear of attack. She served supper to the children while watching the Indians from the window and deciding what to do. After eating, she gathered the children for prayer, and by the time she rose from her knees, she'd made up her mind.

They were going to sleep at the Indian camp. She marched up to the Navajo chief and informed him that the children were afraid and would like to stay with them. "Aren't you Yawgatt's friend?" she asked, using the Navajo name for her husband. The chief agreed.

Brooks said that Emma had planned to stay up all night,

but fell asleep. At dawn, she awoke to find her children safe and the Navajos gone. Later, the chief told another Mormon of the incident, remarking, "Yawgatt's squaw very brave."

Emma was alone again, in October, 1873, when she gave birth to her sixth child, a girl. As she lay in bed, wracked by pain, she prayed that she wouldn't die with five of her youngest children playing happily outside, unaware of her predicament. After the birth, she called for her oldest son, Billy, 12, who was waiting in the kitchen. With his help, she tied the cord and cut it, sprinkled parched flour on the navel, and covered the newborn with olive oil.

Emma asked Billy not to tell the younger kids about their infant sister until supper. She needed an hour to rest. In her journal, Emma wrote: "I've been thinking a lot about my home in Old England these last few days, of the wonderful damp fog and the green grass everywhere and of our wonderful Queen, so I have decided to name the baby Victoria for the Queen, and Elizabeth for her grandmother, Elizabeth Doyle Lee."

The law eventually caught up with John D. Lee. He was found guilty — a scapegoat, many believed — and executed by firing squad on March 23, 1877. His death was photographed by James Fennemore, the man Emma had nursed to health five years earlier.

Emma sold the ferry to the Mormon Church in 1879 and departed Lonely Dell. She was helped in the move by Franklin French, a tall, bearded, Civil War veteran and prospector who headquartered near Emma's place. But she couldn't escape the curse that accompanied the name John D. Lee.

Even though the agreed-upon payment for the ferry was 100 milk cows, she received only 14. Brooks said the experience helped Emma decide to marry French, in Snowflake, Arizona, on August 9, 1879. "He was honorable and honest, and he could defend her interests better than she could herself," Brooks wrote.

French and Emma settled at Brigham City, near Holbrook, but harassment forced them to leave. Their next home, in the White Mountains, was burned in an 1882 Apache uprising. Eventually, she opened a restaurant at Hardy Station, the terminus of the Atlantic and Pacific Railroad, then under construction.

But in these years, Emma is best remembered as a "doctor." The words, "Quick, get Dr. French!" became commonplace in the towns, ranches, and cowboy camps of northern Arizona. She became unofficial physician to railroad workers laying track across empty stretches of the Territory. Many times the railroad company sent a single car to pick her up, take her to a sick worker living in a remote line shack, and bring her home the same day.

"She had no degrees in medicine," wrote Winslow author Vada Carlson. "What she had was an innate knowledge of healing, a few supplies and a little black bag, such as doctors carried, plus a spotlessly white apron."

In Winslow, where she moved in 1887, Grandma French delivered countless babies in the birthing room of her home, known as "the baby farm." She even traveled to remote hogans to help Navajo women, occasionally receiving freshly killed game as payment, and she pitched in when Winslow's saloons delivered wounded customers.

In 1892, a cowboy was shot and another badly cut in a brawl. When the local doctor was sober enough to examine the patients, he pronounced the wounds fatal. "No use to trouble with them," he said. But Emma went to work on the men, and within two weeks both were back sipping drinks at the saloon, side by side.

But even as she helped others, Emma was shadowed by sorrow. In 1888, 14-year-old Victoria Lee, shunned and taunted for being John D.'s daughter, committed suicide by drinking a bottle of laudanum taken from her mother's medicines. Four years later, Emma's son, Ike, was murdered in his Holbrook home by a man who had seduced his wife.

In November, 1897, with Frank French off on a six-month prospecting trip, Emma had troubling premonitions.

She longed for her husband and asked friends who might see him to send him home. On November 16, Frank returned for a joyous reunion. An hour later, as Emma started for the kitchen to cook his favorite meal, her heart gave out. "Oh, Frank!" exclaimed the 61-year-old, slumping to the floor.

As Winslow learned she was dying, businessmen, housewives, Navajos, and even a few prostitutes kept vigil at her home. Crews on passing trains stilled their whistles. The crowd wept and swapped stories about Grandma French until a minister appeared on the porch and declared, "It's over. She has gone."

In her obituary, the *Winslow Mail* wrote that she was "filled to overflowing with the milk of human kindness . . . always ready to respond to the call of the afflicted, whether rich or poor."

After her funeral, nearly every resident of town honored Emma's memory by walking in a procession with her casket to the Winslow cemetery.

Mollie Monroe

*One newspaper headline declared
she was "Fighting Mollie Monroe, the Amazon
of Arizona" whose "cool nerve and
dauntless courage" saved the lives
of 20 scouts. Riled by such newspaper
accounts sensationalizing her eccentricities,
the public condemned Mollie for dressing
and acting like a man and supposedly
being addicted to whiskey.*

———◆———

MOLLIE MONROE DIED A LONESOME AND DISSOLUTE WRECK in Arizona's Territorial Insane Asylum, put there by heartache, revenge, and whiskey. From about age 20 on, they had colored every choice and circumstance of her life.

Her story is a kind of frontier morality play about the self-fulfillment of celebrity, human weakness, and the clash between a woman's choices and the expectations of an American frontier town.

Maybe the disgust Mollie generated among solid pioneer women was due to her penchant for tobacco and dressing like a man, or the way she picked up and dropped husbands so easily. Or maybe the disdain Prescott's ladies showed Cowboy Mollie comes from the fact that she'd once been one of them.

When she arrived in town, between 1864 and 1868, she was said to be the proper wife of an army officer at Fort Whipple, well-bred and well-mannered, a young woman of considerable charm. But when her husband was transferred, Mollie stayed behind, and an inexplicable transformation occurred. She took up the look and — it seemed — the life of a man.

Newspaper accounts describe her riding through town wearing a fringed and beaded buckskin jacket and broad-brimmed hat. She carried a Henry rifle on her saddle, a big knife on her belt, and six-shooters on her hips.

"Strangers to Prescott would invariably take her for a boy dressed in the height of fashion," according to the *Arizona Enterprise* for July 25, 1877, "but would be surprised at the ease and sangfroid with which the supposed boy would call for his whiskey straight, and complacently smoke his Havana."

Mollie wore pants so often that in 1872 the Prescott newspaper considered it newsworthy that she appeared in town in a dress. It was the first time that had happened in seven years.

What drove Mollie's eccentricities most likely was a busted love affair, but much of her early life is not recorded. Even the place of her birth is difficult to confirm. Some sources say New York, others New Hampshire. The 1870 territorial census for Wickenburg says that Mary Monroe, a cook, then 24 and the wife of George Monroe, was born in Mississippi in 1846.

The most often-told story of how Mary E. Sawyer, Mollie's birth name, came West begins with a teenage romance opposed by both sets of parents. The young man reportedly was sent away in the hope, according to Mollie's obituary, that "a long journey would gradually poison" the relationship.

But headstrong Mollie, slightly built, red-haired, and, according to some accounts, the product of a swank finishing school, had other ideas. Two months after her beau's departure, she put on men's clothing and stole away from her parents' home to track down her love.

She traveled under the name Sam Brewer, moving from town to town, at times working with a prospecting party. In Santa Fe, she learned that her man was dead, killed in a barroom brawl only two weeks earlier.

Some accounts say that Mollie then swore allegiance to her lover's memory, vowing to take a life for a life. In disguises ranging from scout to stage driver, she reportedly searched from Salt Lake City to the Mexican border without success.

But the thought of the killers, and what they'd taken away, tortured her. "While under the influence of liquor," wrote the *Arizona Journal-Miner*, "time and again, [she] had been heard to give utterance to her thoughts that carried her back to the days when she was pursuing the object of her hatred."

Mollie met George Monroe sometime before 1870. He was a well-known pioneer and miner who came to Arizona as a soldier in the early 1860s. He and Mollie spent much of their time mining in the Bradshaw Mountains and around Wickenburg. In 1874, he discovered a warm spring south of Prescott and named it Monroe Springs. The place later was called Castle Hot Springs and became a resort drawing tourists from around the country.

George had some success as a miner, and so did Mollie. Press accounts say she discovered two rich gold mines and sold an interest in one of them for $2,500. But within 10 days, she had gambled and boozed her way clear of that fortune. "She was an inveterate gambler," wrote the *Arizona Enterprise*.

The same paper, picking up a wild story originally published in the *San Francisco Mail*, recounted some of her adventures under the headline, "Fighting Mollie Monroe, the Amazon of Arizona."

The newspaper report told of her supposed fondness for riding with army scouts in their hunts for Apaches, and on one occasion, her "cool nerve and dauntless courage" in saving the lives of 20 scouts:

"After a long day's march through the Pinal Mountains, on a fresh trail, we went into a camp on Clear Creek about sundown, and had no more than turned our horses loose and commenced preparing supper, than all at once our camp was surrounded by yelling Indians.

"Already two of our number had bit the dust, and the rest were in a fair way to die or take the alternative of surrendering and being burned at the stake, when Mollie and Texas Johnson, who had lagged a few miles to gather some mescal, appeared on a neighboring hill and began shooting, and at the same time beckoning to another party.

Insane Asylum, Phoenix, Ariz.

**MOLLIE SPENT HER LAST YEARS AT THE
TERRITORIAL INSANE ASYLUM, SHOWN HERE
LOOKING MORE LIKE A RESORT.**

"The ruse had the desired effect, for it threw them [the Indians] into confusion, and gave us a chance to gain the shelter of some bluffs close by. Texas Johnson and Mollie, after some hard fighting, succeeded in reaching us. They had to abandon their horses and fight their way on foot."

Mollie's status as an oddity made her a favorite of the press. The more that newspapers reported her eccentricities the louder were the public's demands to rein her in — on charges of indecent dress, foul language, drunkenness. It might have been that rebel Mollie was flattered by the attention.

According to one story, she was on a prospecting trip with a male companion when the two stopped at a ranch. After her friend went inside, the woman who lived there came out to invite Mollie to dismount and join them.

She did. But when the buckskin-clad visitor answered that her name was Mollie Monroe, revealing her gender, the hostess became indignant. No self-respecting woman dresses in men's clothing, she sniffed.

With a gleam in her eye, Mollie reportedly remarked that

she couldn't prospect in women's clothes. The hostess wasn't swayed, and Mollie was shown the door.

But the buckskin lady won admiration in many quarters, too. She was big-hearted, often taking up collections to help miners and prostitutes in the camps around Prescott and Wickenburg.

"She has been known to ride miles to reach the afflicted," wrote the *Arizona Journal-Miner*, "and with her own means has generously extended help, and without any solicitation whatever."

Mollie once heard of a woman living in desperation with her two children in a mining camp near Wickenburg. Her husband had gone to town to buy supplies, and spent the next three days in a saloon. Mollie and three men found the miner, roped him to a horse, and forced him back to his family. Then they spent the night to make sure the man stayed put.

But those who wished for her downfall eventually got it. Both before and after her time with George Monroe, she went through a string of men without getting near a clergyman, and, according to the *Journal-Miner*, eventually "became addicted to liquor and . . . morals that are dissolute."

In 1877 she was discovered wandering aimlessly in Peeples Valley. Lawman Ed Bowers brought her back to Prescott, where the court, on May 9 of that year, declared her insane and ordered her sent to an asylum in Stockton, California.

The stage carrying Mollie and Bowers was a few miles outside of Wickenburg when it was waylaid by four masked men. Bowers lost $450 in gold coins and a fine watch, but he got Mollie safely to the sanitarium.

After some violent outbursts, including trying to burn the Stockton asylum to the ground, she was reportedly shipped to jail at San Quentin. A year later, she was back at Stockton and taking visits from the likes of A.P.K. Safford, Arizona's ex-governor. She swore to him that her desire to drink was gone and that, if freed, she would never tip another bottle. But it was only a bluff to sway the influential Safford.

A different Mollie emerged two years later, one who, according to the *Arizona Weekly Miner*, still would "resort to any stratagem to obtain a bottle." In the same story, published January 30, 1880, she protested that what doctors were calling her craziness was in fact meanness.

"She said that she was the meanest thing on earth," reported the *Miner*, "and intended to be so until she was turned out and allowed to live as she pleased."

Early in 1887, Mollie was sent to the newly built Territorial asylum near Phoenix. Eight years later, she escaped and eluded pursuers for four days, again giving the press a grand story.

Maricopa County Sheriff Lindley Orme was unable to find her and had to offer a reward to entice Indian trackers to join the search. Then, Mollie was spotted leaving a trading post on the Salt River Reservation, heading into the desert near Telegraph Pass.

Since she was known to have only some crackers and a bottle of water, most assumed that Mollie would be found dead. But she walked 15 miles, barefoot, over rocky terrain and through a cactus forest. She was found with her feet torn and bleeding and her shoes dangling from her wrist.

Newspapers described Mollie's shocking appearance — snow-white hair above the face of a much younger woman — and her elation at escaping, which she expressed with unprintable profanity. "If I had a only had my breeches and my gun I'd a been all right," she boasted to the *Arizona Republican*.

But it was her last hurrah. The woman whose consuming desire for revenge made her life a public spectacle was returned to the asylum, where she died in 1902, after a quarter century of confinement.

CHAPTER ELEVEN

Olive Oatman

*At 13, she saw Indians bludgeon to death
her father, mother, and four siblings on the
Arizona desert west of Tucson. But her horror
was just beginning. For five years, Indians
enslaved her, often torturing her.
Amid public gawking after her deliverance,
she remained "delicate, lady-like and courteous,"
according to a newspaper account.*

———◈———

THE MASSACRE BY INDIANS OF SIX MEMBERS OF THE OATMAN family, and the subsequent enslavement of Olive Oatman, is a story of almost biblical dimension. When the details were revealed in the *Los Angeles Star* in April, 1856, and later in a best-selling book, Americans gasped. The horror seemed unreal, and it expanded over time in various re-tellings, eventually acquiring the status of myth

But it was true — the terrible murders, ravenous wolves, a killing famine, a crucifixion, and, in the middle of it, a girl of sweet innocence forced to live out her days with five blue lines tattooed on her chin, the symbol of her captors.

The story even has a last supper. It occurred the evening of February 18, 1851, when the Oatmans gathered on a lonesome mesa, 80 miles east of Yuma, to eat dry bread and bean soup.

The family's journey to that place began in Illinois. They were followers of a Mormon sect led by James C. Brewster. He claimed he had divine guidance to lead his people to a land called Bashan, in the southwestern portion of what now is Arizona. But by the time the Brewster group reached New Mexico, bickering had divided them and changed their goals.

Brewster led one party north toward the Santa Fe Trail, never making it to Bashan. Eventually, he established his community near Socorro Peak, New Mexico.

Roys Oatman, a headstrong farmer, led a second party onto Cooke's wagon road to the Gila Trail, straight through Tucson and Apacheria. The danger was great. But by then, Oatman also had abandoned hope of reaching Bashan. His new dream was to get rich in California's gold fields — apparently without regard to the risk it posed to his wife and seven children.

His group of eight wagons reached Tucson in mid-January, 1851, but just barely. They had lost horses and valuable stores of beans to Apache raiders, and their oxen were so close to dropping that wagons and baggage had to be abandoned. The travelers survived by eating hawks, coyote soup, and biscuits. After a short rest, Oatman packed up again, this time with only two families — the Kellys and Wilders — willing to follow.

His wagon train pressed north through what Jesuit writer Edward J. Pettid called "the 90-mile desert," past Picacho Peak to Casa Grande, the Pima villages and Maricopa Wells. Friendly Indians warned the travelers that Apaches were rampaging along the Gila Trail and that to continue was foolhardy. The Kellys and Wilders were convinced.

But Oatman still believed he could make it to Fort Yuma on the Colorado River. He was encouraged by Dr. John Lawrence LeConte, a respected entomologist nicknamed "Dr. Bugs." He had just completed work on the Gila River and said he'd seen no Indians.

Based on this report, but with little food and weakened animals, the Oatmans set out again on February 11. The going was hard, and the family's condition worsened. Four days later, as LeConte was returning to California, he passed the Oatman camp. Roys gave the doctor a letter pleading with Fort Yuma's commander for food, harness, and strong animals.

"Honorable Sir," he wrote, "I am under the necessity of calling upon you for assistance. There is myself, my wife and seven children, and without help we must perrish [sic]."

About 30 miles west of their meeting place, LeConte and his guide were set upon by Apaches and robbed of their horses. Before continuing on foot, "Dr. Bugs" scribbled a letter and posted it to a tree beside the trail, warning the Oatmans of the danger. But they missed it, and on Tuesday, February 18, the family camped on a quiet mesa near the Gila River and prepared to eat supper.

The approaching Indians at first appeared friendly, asking for tobacco and food. Then they attacked. Olive, who was 13 at the time, recalled the horror years later:

"I saw them strike Lorenzo down and in an instant, my father also. I was so bewildered and surprised that it was some little time before I could realize the full horror of the situation. . . . I saw my father, my own dear father, struggling, bleeding and moaning in the most pitiful manner.

"Lorenzo was lying with his face in the dust with the top of his head covered with blood. I looked around and saw my poor dear mother lying on the ground with the baby clasped in her arms; both of them were still as if the work of death had been completed. I then heard my poor bleeding mangled mother utter a moan, and I sprang wildly towards her. The Indian standing over me snatched me back."

What Olive spoke of was butchery. Using war clubs, 19 Yavapais bludgeoned six Oatmans to death — Roys, wife Mary Ann, pregnant with her eighth child, and children Lucy, Roys Jr., C.A., and an unnamed baby.

The lucky one, 14-year-old Lorenzo, later awoke with blood pouring from his mouth and ears. As he struggled back toward Maricopa Wells, he was trailed by wolves that had caught the scent of his blood, and he was nearly shot in an encounter with more Indians. The Wilders and Kellys eventually rescued him.

After removing Olive's shoes and stripping her of nearly all her clothing, the Yavapais pushed her and her 7-year-old sister Mary Ann on a course to the north. They ran through the night, roped together. "We did not sleep," Olive said. "We prayed all night."

FOR THE REST OF HER LIFE, OLIVE OATMAN WORE THE BLUE CHIN TATOO OF HER MOHAVE CAPTIVITY.

Travel was continuous the next day, the dust and thirst nearly choking them to death. If Olive lagged behind, she was beaten. When she and Mary Ann pleaded for rest and water, the Indians cackled and pricked them with lances. Olive estimated they traveled 100 miles before reaching the Indian camp, near present-day Congress, her lacerated feet sprinkling blood on the ground the whole way.

More horrors awaited at the rancheria. "The squaws and children would beat us with rods and get coals of fire and make us stand on them," Olive said in *Arizona Graphic* magazine for October 28, 1899. "The children would take long sticks, put one end into the fire so that they would have a coal on and prick us with those firebrands. Torture was no name for it. Death would have been sweet in comparison."

But the long nightmare was only beginning. The Yavapais

forced the Oatman girls to perform backbreaking labor and clubbed them if their pace slowed. Eventually, the tribe traded the girls to Mohave Indians for a few pounds of beads, two horses, and two blankets. In the 10-day trek north to the Mohave villages — on the Colorado opposite Needles — the girls were forced to march "like horses," again barefoot. Olive told the *Star* they were fed only once, a slice of meat about the size of her hand.

"Not an act of kindness, nor a word of sympathy or hope had been addressed to her by her captors, who treated her and her sister as slaves," reported the *Star*.

But that changed on arrival. The girls were taken in as family by Chief Espanesay and given blankets, food, and seeds to raise their own corn, beans, and melon. They also were tatooed on the chin in the tribal sign, the ki-e-chook. The chief's wife, whose name is absent from historical accounts, took a motherly interest in Olive and probably saved her life during a severe drought and subsequent famine in 1853. She parted with some of her precious seed corn, grinding it into a gruel for Olive to eat.

But little Mary Ann wasn't as strong as Olive, and like numerous Mohaves, she slowly wasted away. One night, as death neared, the girls sat holding hands and singing hymns their mother had taught them. At one point, Mary Ann looked into her sister's eyes and said, "I have been a great deal of trouble to you, Olive. You will miss me for awhile, but you will not have to work so hard when I am gone."

Another horror, reported by several sources, occurred when Mohave warriors returned from a war party with a Cocopah captive named Nowercha. In fighting between the two tribes, she was separated from her baby and wanted desperately to return. She escaped from the Mohave village, dove into the Colorado River, and began swimming to the south. But the Mohaves recaptured Nowercha, returned her to their village, and crucified her.

As she hung, secured to the cross by coarse wooden pegs driven through her hands and feet, the entire tribe danced around, singing and shooting arrows into her. Olive and other captives were forced to watch, a warning should they consider getting away.

Release came in early 1856. A Mohave named Francisco brought word to Fort Yuma that Olive was being held by the tribe. The commander sent Francisco back to the Mohaves with a letter demanding her release in exchange for four blankets, white beads, some trinkets, and a horse.

When she walked up to the fort on February 22, 1856, Olive was so embarrassed by her spare bark skirt that she buried herself in sand until clothes were brought. Her skin was badly sunburned, making it difficult to tell if she really was white. Only by lifting her hair and inspecting behind her ears could fort personnel be sure. When an interpreter asked her name, she drew her finger through the loose ground, spelling out Olive Oatman.

Lorenzo had spent five years refusing to give up hope that his sisters were alive, even mounting search missions. When he read of Olive's release, he rushed to her side, creating a sensation of press interest that mushroomed when the two returned to California. Amid the swirl of attention, including crowds gawking at Olive, the *Star* wrote that she remained "delicate, lady-like and courteous."

In 1857, Royal B. Stratton, a California minister, published a book about the Oatman girls. It sold 30,000 copies in two years and drew good reviews. On reading of the Indians' treatment of the girls, one newspaper wrote, "The American people ought to go out and give them a good whipping."

A question that consumed many observers was whether Olive had been sexually abused by her captors. In Stratton's book, she said, "To the honor of those savages let it be said, they never offered the least unchaste abuse to me." Writers of the day believed her, perhaps wishfully. The denial upheld her reputation for innocence, as well as contemporary standards, which had little tolerance for intimacy between a white woman and an Indian.

But historian Richard Dillon, writing in *American West* magazine in 1981, reported that a close friend of Olive's from the wagon journey stated flatly that she'd been the wife of the Mohave chief's son and bore him two boys. Susan Thompson's source for that revelation was Olive herself. Even today, the question has never been definitively answered.

In November of 1865, Olive married John B. Fairchild. Among the myths that grew up around her was the belief, often stated and even published, that she died in a New York insane asylum in 1877. But she and John, a prominent banker, adopted a baby girl, Mamie, and lived for more than 30 years in Sherman, Texas.

"She was very shy and retiring, probably due to the blue tattoo around her mouth," recalled Sherman resident Katherine Brents Collie in an interview with author Edward Pettid. "When she went to town, she always wore a dark veil. She was very slender and walked with great dignity."

Memories of her captivity must've tormented Olive's later life. Some reported that she spent long nights pacing the floor and weeping, perhaps, say believers of Thompson's story, at the loss of her Mohave babies. And at the time of their marriage, Fairchild bought and burned every available copy of Stratton's book. We can assume he was behaving as a dutiful husband, helping his wife forget what no veil could erase.

Olive was delivered from her second captivity by a heart attack in 1903. She was 65.

CHAPTER TWELVE

Larcena Pennington

*The frontier's harshest elements could not defeat
this woman, born in Tennessee, raised in Texas,
and tempered in Arizona. After Apache Indians
abducted her, they tortured her and left
her for dead. But she survived. Apaches killed
her husband, father, and two brothers.
But she endured. And she recovered
from the dreaded smallpox.*

━━━◆◆◆━━━

THE ARIZONA TERRITORY'S HISTORY HAS MUCH TO SAY
about lawmen such as Wyatt Earp and heroes of the
Apache wars such as chief of scouts Al Sieber. These
and others are figures of unquestioned bravery. But it might
be time to add Larcena Pennington to the list.

She was 23 years old in 1860 when Apaches kidnapped
and tortured her and left her for dead. In subsequent days —
battered, bloody, and almost naked — she struggled through the
snowy Santa Rita Mountains to safety.

The ordeal was horrible. But horrible, too, was watching as the frontier claimed one Pennington after another. In
an eight-year period in the 1860s, Larcena lost two sisters to
disease and her husband, father, and two brothers to Apaches.

Surely it would have been easier to pack a wagon and
get out, rather than to continue digging graves. Many of her relatives did just that and fled to Texas. But Larcena stayed. She
endured for 56 years, becoming a quiet symbol of pioneer
strength. At the end of her life, she was described as sweet-
natured and happy, unburdened by the suffering in her past.

The Pennington family, headed by Elias and Julia Ann, began its journey west from farmland near Nashville, Tennessee, where Larcena was born on January 10, 1837. The family settled in Fannin County, Texas. Elias worked as a farmer and freighter while his family grew to 12 children — eight girls and four boys.

After 15 years, Elias' desire to escape encroaching neighbors led him to seek another home. While he was off exploring land 150 miles to the southwest, Julia Ann died. The family moved again before Elias decided, early in 1857, to leave Texas. The 13 Penningtons joined a wagon train headed for California.

The family crossed New Mexico Territory, which until 1863 encompassed Arizona, and forded the San Pedro River, probably south of present-day Benson. They reached Fort Buchanan on Sonoita Creek in June, 1857.

The Penningtons would go no farther. Their animals were exhausted and, according to a sketch of the family written in 1919 by Robert H. Forbes, Larcena needed to recover from what was called "mountain fever." Elias and his sons got a government contract to supply hay to the fort, and his daughters sewed for the soldiers.

The Penningtons, who lived at Fort Buchanan two years, were the first family of U.S. citizenship to settle in Arizona. While at the fort, Larcena met and later married lumberman John Hempstead Page. The wedding, on December 24, 1859, was the first by U.S. citizens in Tucson, then an adobe village populated mostly by Mexicans.

Eleven weeks later, Larcena was with John at his woodcutting camp in the Santa Rita Mountains south of Tucson. Also there was William Randall, John's partner, and 11-year-old Mercedes Sais Quiroz, the adopted daughter of the lumber company's owner.

On the morning of March 16, John left camp to put some laborers to work, and Randall went deer hunting. The first sign of trouble was the sound of a dog barking. Then came a scream from Mercedes. When Larcena looked up from her laundry, she saw the Apaches running toward her.

"Having a six-shooter in my hand," said Larcena in her account, published in the *Missouri Republican*, May 8, 1860, "I turned to fire at them, but they were already so close that before I could pull the trigger they had rushed upon me and seized the weapon."

One of the five raiders, probably the leader, told Larcena that they'd just killed her husband at a nearby spring. She wailed, but stopped when a brave threatened her with a lance to her breast. The raiders looted the camp and, in Larcena's words, "marched us off, hand in hand, in a hurried and barbarous manner."

Writer Forbes, Larcena's son-in-law, wrote that she quickly began tearing off bits of clothing and bending twigs to mark a trail for rescuers. But when the kidnappers saw what she and little Mercedes were doing, they separated the two. The Apaches forced Larcena to march throughout the day over rocky terrain, sapping her strength. After 16 miles, she fell so far behind the that Apaches decided to kill her.

"They stripped me of my clothing, including my shoes, and left me but a single garment," she said. "Then they thrust their lances at me, inflicting 11 wounds in my body, threw me over a ledge of rocks . . . some 16 or 18 feet high, and hurled large stones after me . . . and then left me, supposing that I must die."

Miraculously, Larcena survived. Forbes reported that when she regained consciousness, she heard rescuers on the trail above her. Among the voices was her husband's, declaring: "Here it is, boys!" He was referring to the tracks left by her shoes, which one of the Apaches had put on. Larcena yelled, but she was so weak, her cry did not reach them.

After the men departed, following the false trail, Larcena slipped back into unconsciousness. Days later she revived, weak from the loss of blood, and applied snow to her wounds. Then, barefoot and wearing only a petticoat, she began her

**AN ARIZONA RESIDENT FOR 56 YEARS,
LARCENA PENNINGTON OUTLASTED
THE REST OF HER FAMILY.**

impossible journey home. Before the end of the first day, her feet "gave up" and she was forced to crawl through the mountains.

"Sometimes, after crawling up a steep ledge," she said, "laboring hard for half a day, I would lose my grasp and slide down lower than the place from which I started."

She ate grass and drank melted snow. At night, she slept in holes scratched in the sand. In the morning, she waited for the warmth of the day before setting out again, but the sun blistered her bare shoulders.

On the 14th day, Larcena reached a recently deserted workmen's camp, its fire still smoldering. She rekindled it and by gathering some flour that had spilled on the ground, made some bread — the first food she'd eaten since the kidnapping.

"I was now near the workmen in the pinery [forest] and within two miles of my home," she said, "but was too weak to go on. I could hear the men at work and sometimes saw them, but could not attract their attention."

The next morning, Larcena began crawling again. She reached a road cutting through the woods and waited until workmen came upon her.

Forbes wrote: "With clotted hair and gaping wounds, nearly naked, emaciated and sunburned, she was at first mistaken for an unfortunate outcast squaw, and the men ran for their guns."

Larcena was taken to a doctor in Tucson and reunited with John Page. What a shock it must have been. She was a skeleton and, according to one description, her lips stretched so tightly against her jaw that the teeth were visible through them.

The kidnappers kept Mercedes because she was light enough to carry. She was later returned to Fort Buchanan in a prisoner swap.

The story of Larcena's ordeal drew gasps from newspaper readers, who proclaimed her a heroine and her survival a miracle.

This happy ending didn't end Larcena's hardships. In the spring of 1861, her husband was killed by Apaches while he was freighting toward Fort Breckenridge, northeast of Tucson. John Page was buried where he fell and Larcena never saw him again. Forbes said she was given only "his handkerchief, his purse and a lock of his hair." At the time, Larcena was three month's pregnant.

She moved into her father's house on the Santa Cruz River. But with the Apaches warring, and Army troops pulling out to fight the Civil War, no place in southern Arizona was safe. Most settlers packed their wagons, but Elias Pennington refused to leave.

"I have as much right here as the Indians," he said.

He moved his family, including Larcena, into a fortified mine near Patagonia. In September, 1861, under a siege led by Cochise and beset by an outbreak of smallpox, Larcena gave birth to her first child, Mary Ann. Stories of the Penningtons' time there tell of Sylvester Mowry, the mine operator, treating the disease by keeping sufferers, including Larcena and the baby, on a flour-and-water diet that nearly starved them. But most of the stricken recovered.

The next years for the Penningtons were violent and terrible. The men continued cutting wood at Madera Canyon, in the Santa Ritas, and hauling it to the sawmill at Tubac or to the Cerro Colorado mine. They also operated a sawmill in Tucson on land that would become Pennington Street, one of downtown's main avenues.

While the men worked, the women remained at home, alone. The danger was always extreme. Pioneer Charley B. Genung recalled visiting Tubac in April, 1864, and finding the town abandoned. Only the Pennington women, their two young brothers, and Larcena and her baby, lived there.

"Every morning," wrote Forbes, "the two boys, with guns as long as themselves, carefully reconnoitered each side of the path to the spring from which the women then carried the water supply for the day."

The family moved often, seeking safety. But death stalked them. In 1867, Larcena's sister, Ann, died of malaria. The next year, brother Jim was killed while pursuing Apaches who had stolen oxen from his camp near the San Xavier Mission, south of Tucson. And in June, 1869, Elias and son Green were ambushed and killed while working at their farm on Sonoita Creek.

After these deaths, Forbes reported, the remaining Pennington sisters, along with a younger brother and Larcena's daughter, Mary Ann Page, traveled to Tucson and prepared to go to California. But even their escape was marred by death. They were only 20 miles outside of Tucson when Ellen, the eldest Pennington daughter, fell ill. The train turned back to Tucson, and she died of pneumonia there.

For brother Jack Pennington, that was enough. He traveled to Arizona and brought what remained of his family back to Texas to live with him. Larcena was the only one to remain. In August, 1870, she married a Scottish-born lawyer and judge named William Fisher Scott. Their wedding announcement, published in the *Weekly Arizonian*, is considered a classic:

"Wm. Scott, Esq., of the firm of Lee and Scott of this place, after having withstood the dangers and hardships of about twelve years of frontier life, and reached a standard of prosperity which most men might envy, was last week — not killed by Apaches, as the reader may suppose, but on the contrary quite otherwise — united in marriage to a most excellent lady, a daughter of the late Mr. Pennington, a lady who, individually and in connection with her family, has already figured prominently in the history of the early settler in Arizona."

Larcena had two more children, son William and daughter Georgie, and lived the remainder of her life in Tucson. They were good and nourishing years. She was among the first members of the Congregational Church in Tucson and, fittingly, president of the Society of Arizona Pioneers, later renamed the Arizona Historical Society. At a celebration marking the Scotts' 37th anniversary in 1907, *The Tucson Post* described Larcena as "tall, white-haired, dignified, sustained by an overruling providence to pass her declining years in tenderness and peace."

She earned those comforts and her "good death" on March 31, 1913, at age 76. But there remains a question for which no answer is evident: Why, after such suffering, after Arizona's ground had been soaked with the blood of her kin, did she stay in the Territory? None of the stories written about her, or related memoirs, offers any clues, and Larcena never explained, leaving to us the formidable task of measuring the heart of a pioneer.

CHAPTER THIRTEEN

Mary Post

*A broken romance drove her away from
a safe and proper life in the East. To escape,
she went West, becoming only the fifth educator
to teach in the Arizona Territory. For more than
four decades, she taught generations of youth
in Yuma and tirelessly maintained efforts
to civilize the raw frontier.*

W HEN MARY ELIZABETH POST STEPPED DOWN FROM THE stage coach that spring day in 1872, she didn't feel much like a princess. The long journey from San Diego had layered her clothing with dust. The sight of Arizona City (later renamed Yuma), with its mud huts and naked Indian men, surely sent a shiver up the back of this well-bred New York teacher.

She must have recalled the conversation she'd had a few days before with friend John G. Capron, operator of a stage line that ran from San Diego to Mesilla, New Mexico, a distance of 800 miles. He had heard of a teaching job in Ehrenberg, up the Colorado River from Arizona City, and told Mary about it.

"Is it perfectly safe and proper," she asked, "for a young, unmarried woman to go to Arizona alone?"

Capron laughed. "I assure you that any lady who goes to Arizona and conducts herself as a lady will be treated like a princess."

The 30-year-old teacher, the fifth to come to Arizona Territory, was taken to a private residence where two other teachers lived. She got an initiation when she tried to wash up.

The water, delivered in buckets that had been dipped into the Colorado, was laden with a heavy, red silt that clung to clothing and flesh. Only after the dirt had settled was the water usable.

But Mary shed no tears at her predicament. She had come willingly to this remote place — not so much to test herself as an educator as to escape a relationship. The story of her broken engagement to an Iowa politician is central in her life, but it is difficult to understand. Even her biographer, Ruth Leedy Gordon, was hard-pressed to explain how a campaign lie — that Mary's man was having an affair — could separate two lovers for a lifetime, even after the truth had been revealed.

Mary was hostage to pride and her upbringing. She was born on a farm in Elizabethtown, New York, across Lake Champlain southwest of Burlington, Vermont, on June 17, 1841. Her father, a carpenter who read the works of editor Horace Greeley, raised his eight children in a literate and socially conscious environment. The Underground Railroad, which spirited slaves to freedom, was running at the time, and the Post home often served as an overnight way-station for blacks on their way to Canada.

Mary's first education was in public schools. But her father thought the seven-month term was too short and hired a tutor for an additional three months of study. Mary got her first teaching job in 1856, at age 15. Several years later, when she tried to attend the University of Vermont in Burlington, she found the school didn't admit girls, so she enrolled at Burlington Female Seminary. Mary moved west with her family after graduating in July, 1863.

She was living in Allamakee County, Iowa, when rumors about her fiancé, a rising young politician unnamed in Gordon's biography, gained wide currency. Mary's hurt was so deep she withdrew, refusing even to answer her love's letter. He called on her, and still she refused to speak. Gordon wrote that the man "picked up his handsome campaign hat and scarf, and strode out of her home."

To escape, Mary took a job teaching in Lansing, Iowa.

But she couldn't forget. While there, she made quiet inquiries into the alleged affair and learned it was a political lie. But even with that knowledge, she couldn't bring herself to apologize or explain.

"Ladies were ladies in those days, and Mary Elizabeth was still very Vermontish," wrote Gordon, who completed her unpublished biography of Post, *Portrait of a Teacher*, in the mid-1930s. "She had enshrined his personality for so long, however, that she could not escape from the spell in which she was held, so she decided to go further west and try again to forget in newer surroundings."

She arrived in San Diego in January, 1872, and traveled from there to Yuma in a "mud wagon."

"To call it a stage would be decidedly misrepresenting the facts," said Mary, in a profile in *Progressive Arizona* magazine in 1926. With two other passengers crowded in, she was forced to sit upright for 48 hours, stopping only to change horses and for meals — usually crackers, bacon, black coffee, and "Arizona strawberries," a term the drivers used for beans.

The worst of the journey came after the wagon descended the San Diego Mountains and began the long ride across the desert. "Not without some misgivings did we drive out onto the plains that . . . night in April, with a refreshing wind at our back," she said. "Before the sun had fully set, a dust storm overtook our wagon and nearly stampeded the horses before they could be turned with their backs to the cutting wind."

Close to dawn, the driver lost the road, and the passengers insisted that he stop. Mary and the others jumped down and gathered mesquite for a bonfire. The blaze cheered them until sunrise, when they rediscovered the road and pressed on.

After a short stay in Yuma, Mary traveled by steamship to Ehrenberg. She was met there by Governor A.P.K. Safford, who helped her open, in an old saloon, the Territory's third public school. It had no windows, there was an earthen floor, and classes occasionally were visited by bleary-eyed miners looking for a drink.

**THIS 1907 SHOT OF THE YUMA WOMEN'S CLUB
SHOWS MARY POST, THE WHITE-HAIRED WOMAN
SEATED FIFTH FROM THE RIGHT.**

Six months later, in the fall of 1872, Mary returned to Yuma. With the exception of two school terms taught elsewhere, she spent the next 40 years there, often teaching generations of the same family and becoming the town's most tireless advocate for civilization.

But the early years were hard. As a single white woman among Indians and Mexicans, she was a curiosity. "I never but once went out on the street unaccompanied," she told *Progressive Arizona*, "and then I was stared at from windows and doorways."

Mary's high standards drew protests from parents. She insisted on regular attendance, and when students failed to show up, she went to their homes and got them. Classes were held in one room of a private home. To improve her students' dress, she sent to San Francisco for clothing in the Butterick pattern and went door to door teaching her pupils' mothers to cut cloth for clothes. Author Gordon called it the first home-extension education in the public schools of Arizona.

Even with these few trappings of modern life, Yuma still was frontier. It brimmed with excited talk of bonanza mines and men with big appetites for money and trouble. One of them, Manuel Fernandez, murdered a local merchant and was ordered to the gallows for Arizona's first legal hanging, an incident that Mary's Eastern sensitivities found hard to accept.

On the morning of May 2, 1873, she went to class as always. But with the gallows directly across from school and a crowd clamoring to watch Fernandez swing, she had no choice but to cancel class and send her pupils home.

The atmosphere disturbed her, and it worsened after the hanging. The *Arizona Sentinel* newspaper, commenting on the actions of a San Diego judge, who, instead of sending criminals to jail, sentenced them to go to Arizona, suggested that vigilantes meet the judge's exiles at the Territory's border and deal with them there. The brutish climate alarmed Mary so much that she accepted a job as vice principal of San Diego's schools.

Within a year, she was back in Yuma, drawn by a decision of school trustees to split the students, putting Mary in charge of the girls and hiring Albert Post, her brother, to take the boys. With the completion of a new courthouse, the old courthouse and jail would be used as classrooms. Mary considered this better than previous accommodations, although the crude etchings by the prisoners still were visible on the jail walls.

Albert's arrival made Mary's life more pleasurable. She was able to venture outside more often, and the time spent indoors was enlivened by music, thanks to the organ her brother purchased in San Francisco,

Albert also was good friends with Mary's former fiancé and often received letters from him. The handwriting and the Iowa postmarks quickened Mary's heart. But it sank when Albert told her, time after time in response to her inquiries, that she wasn't mentioned in the letters.

Teaching was Mary's refuge. She fought to get supplies for her students, once strong-arming a prominent citizen into holding a horse race that raised $600 for textbooks. Another time she sent river captain Isaac Polhamus into Yuma's streets to collect money for a Christmas pageant. He returned in a hour with $500 gathered from businessmen and miners.

Mary entered several political battles on the side of women's suffrage and as a tepid supporter of prohibition. She rarely was righteous in her beliefs, but she could burn with indignation when her school was threatened. Gordon wrote of an incident in which a man tried to take Mary's job as principal by electing school trustees who agreed that she was partial to Mexicans. Yuma was an American city, the man argued, and deserved a principal who cared for American students.

The night before the election, the man went to El Rincon, a Mexican neighborhood, and handed out slips of paper naming his candidates, and these were to be used for ballots the next day. Until that time, Mary had paid little attention to the campaign against her, but his trick stirred her anger. "Such people must not get control of our schools," she declared. "I shall take up the matter in the morning."

The next day, she hired a wagon and went from house to house in El Rincon, picking up Mexican women. She knew most of them personally, had taught their children, and had been in their homes instructing them how to cook and sew. All day, she went back and forth from the neighborhood to the polling place until every Rincon woman had voted, thwarting her opponent's effort.

By the time she retired at age 72, Mary was such a revered figure that a senator, concerned for her well-being, pushed through the state's first teacher pension bill. It paid her $50 a month. After retirement, she operated a millinery store out of her home, and went door to door in town and to outlying ranches. She sold corsets, taught sewing, and passed out magazines containing serial stories that women enjoyed reading. She never made much money, but she found great satisfaction in spreading her passions for style and culture.

At her death in 1934, at age 93, Mary was hailed as one of the foremost teachers of the western frontier, a woman whose work left an indelible mark on the character of Yuma. "Nothing ever just happens in this world," Mary once said of her call to teach. "I was born and educated for my work . . . There's a divinity that shapes our ends, though hew them as we may."

Mary's other passion, her lost love, remained lost. After Albert's death in 1886, she subscribed to an Iowa newspaper to try to keep track of the man she almost married. But if we are shaped from above, as Mary believed, what divinity would consign to a woman of such great gifts the task of running her finger down columns of type, for years on end, in search of a single name.

CHAPTER FOURTEEN

Viola Slaughter

A great-great-granddaughter of Daniel Boone
and the daughter of a Missouri River boat
captain and a pampered Southerner,
Viola headstrongly married a cattleman.
When he wanted to quit, Viola wouldn't allow it,
and their ranch, the San Bernadino, became one
of the biggest and most prosperous in Arizona.

O NLY THROUGH THE FORCE OF HER WILL DID CORA VIOLA
Howell get the life she wanted. If she had listened to her
mother, a prim Southerner pampered by her slaves,
Viola never would have married Texas cattleman John Horton
Slaughter, who, at 37, was 19 years her senior. His first wife
had died of smallpox the year before, leaving him with two
children, Addie, 6, and Willie, 19 months.

None of that mattered to Viola. The two met at the Howell
ranch, 60 miles south of Roswell, New Mexico. John Slaughter
was awaiting the arrival of some cattle his brother was driving
from Texas. By the time the herd showed up, John had talked
Viola's father into abandoning the farm and starting over in
Arizona.

"I rode much of the way west beside Mr. Slaughter," said
Viola in a 1937 interview. "It was love at first sight."

She vowed to marry the slightly built cowboy, but her
mother, Mary Ann Howell, wouldn't hear of it. Viola went to
her father and told him that she and John planned to ride ahead
to the little town of Tularosa and get hitched. "He was on our
side and said he would tell mother," Viola told her interviewer.

"She cried and had hysterics all that night, but the next day we did as planned."

The wedding took place April 16, 1879. The union became a frontier love story.

During their marriage, he was a tough, two-term sheriff of wild Cochise County, but a man tender enough to bring his wife wildflowers that he'd picked on the range. She laid out his clothes every morning and spoke often of her dependence on his strength. But when his gambling posed a threat to the family, Viola was firm, insisting that he curb his addiction to poker. Together they deveoped one of Arizona's storied ranches, the San Bernardino, east of Douglas.

Born in Missouri on September 18, 1860, Viola Howell was the great-great-granddaughter of Daniel Boone. Her father, Amazon, was a Missouri River boat captain when he joined the Confederacy. He fought to the war's end and was captured and imprisoned nine times.

With hostilities over, the family roamed the West seeking to rebuild their lives. Amazon did whatever he could to make money — farming, washing gold, running a restaurant. The Howells lived in New Mexico during the Lincoln County War, giving Viola a close look at a man soon to become infamous. Billy the Kid stopped at the Howell ranch one day with three other men.

"They leaned their guns against the fireplace and talked with us," Viola told reporter Bernice Cosulich in a story published in *The Arizona Daily Star* in 1938. "Several times later they called, and we came to like handsome Billy."

The Slaughters arrived in Arizona's Sulphur Springs Valley in 1879, and soon they were living in a two-room house with a dirt floor on the San Pedro River. Addie and Willie joined the Slaughter and Howell families, but their visit was supposed to be temporary. To calm Mary Howell's misgivings, Slaughter promised to send his kids to Texas, to be reared by his brother. But Viola's heart wouldn't allow it.

"I became so attached to them in just a few days that I began to dread the time when I must give them up," she said.

**VIOLA SLAUGHTER WEATHERED MANY FRIGHTS
DURING LIFE ON A RANCH.**

"Finally [I] broke down and cried. . . . I don't want them to go. I want to keep them." John, as usual, bowed to his wife's wishes.

In various interviews and reminiscences compiled late in life, Viola acknowledged that she spent the early years of her marriage scared witless — "I was even afraid gopher mounds were graves" — as she and John built their cattle business. In 1880, they opened a market in Charleston, a mill town south of Tombstone, and John had contracts to supply beef to railroads and to soldiers at San Carlos.

Viola accompanied him on trips into Apache territory. "I was dreadfully afraid of the Indians," she said. "When they would try to stop us to beg for tobacco, I made Mr. Slaughter throw it out to them while still moving."

In the winter of 1881, John, Addie, Viola, and her brother, Stonewall, rode the train to New Mexico to bring back more of his cattle. After joining the herd and beginning the trek home, the Slaughters encountered a three-day blizzard in the mountains west of Fort Bayard.

"We wrapped Addie in a big buffalo robe in the bottom of the light wagon, which I drove, and she was the only one out of the 17 of us who escaped having some part of her frozen," Viola said. "Mr Slaughter had an ear and I had a foot frozen. We had no tents or shelter and often in the morning we could hardly turn over for the snow on us."

At another time in Arizona, outlaws were the problem. John and Viola were riding in a wagon from Charleston to Calabasas when three mounted ruffians appeared on a rise ahead. "I grabbed the reins and the whip and started right for them," she said. "I whispered to Mr. Slaughter to get his gun and he answered calmly, 'Why, Viola, I saw them. I have my gun.' . . . To our great surprise, those three bandits turned tail and ran."

In 1883, the Slaughters sold their cattle and headed north to fulfill John's dream of owning a ranch in Oregon on the Snake River. They got as far as Idaho when John, who suffered from asthma and tuberculosis, began hemorrhaging. They turned back and that same year purchased the San Bernardino Mexican land grant.

The giant, 65,000-acre property began in Arizona Territory's southeast Cochise County and ranged into Mexico. Author Reba Wells, writing in the *Journal of Arizona History*, reported that John paid $1.25 an acre and had to borrow part of the money. The land, including a dilapidated hacienda, had been abandoned by the original owners some 50 years before because of Apache raids.

"I shall never forget that first sight of the ranch," Viola said, "the valley stretching far out before us down into Mexico, rimmed and bounded by mountains all around. Nor shall I forget the thrill of knowing that it was all ours, our future lay within it. It was beautiful."

But the early years were lean. The Slaughters weathered a falling beef market and an earthquake in 1887 that flattened every building on the property. They lived in Tombstone during John's years as sheriff (1886-1890). When his last term expired, he announced that he wasn't returning to the rigors of ranch living.

Viola wouldn't hear of it. She told her husband: "We'll go out there and put our shoulders to the wheel. We can't give up now and I can help . . . just you give me a plain house with wide board floors, muslin ceilings and board finish around the adobes. That's all I want."

They moved permanently to the San Bernardino in 1892. Viola's duties as a ranch wife covered just about everything, including doctoring cowboys. They rode in from New Mexico for her treatments. She also accompanied John on trips, helping on one occasion to bring in a murderer. When John needed to drive cattle out of Mexico, Viola hauled her saddle onto the train and rode as far as Hermosillo, then returned with the herd. She was an accomplished horsewoman.

In an interview in the 1920s with pioneer chronicler Charles Morgan Wood, Viola told of hearing that John had been killed by Apaches in Mexico. Despite reports that Indians were planning to raid the ranch, Viola got a wagon and whipped her team toward the border. After three days, she finally saw her husband riding toward her. Her relief was so profound that she grew sick and thought she might topple from the wagon. But she didn't want her husband to see her that way.

"By the time Mr. Slaughter rode up I was sitting up, straight as a ramrod," Viola told Wood.

In addition to caring for Addie and Willie, the Slaughters raised several other children, castaways that fortune assigned to them. One was an Apache baby that John retrieved from Mexico. He'd gone there in pursuit of a renegade band that had killed settlers in southern Arizona in 1896, one of the last such attacks on record.

Apache May — named for the month she was found —

wore a dress made from a political campaign poster. It hung as a wall decoration in Alfred Hands' Chiricahua Mountain ranch when the renegades murdered him. Sewn into the poster, in large black type, were the names of Republican party officials.

Newspapermen speculated that May would grow up wild and turn on her new parents. That never happened, of course. The little celebrity, a bright and loving girl, died on the ranch in 1900 when her dress caught fire as she played near a pot of boiling water.

As time went on, the Slaughters worked their way to considerable affluence. The ranch production reached a peak of 10,000 saleable cattle a year.

Wells describes Viola sleeping late and dressing for dinner, pleasures few ranch women enjoyed. Using linens and china, servants laid out lavish meals consisting of fresh vegetables, jams and preserves, cream, and sides of beef from the cold storage. Rules of the dining room prohibited spurs at the table for men and divided skirts for women.

The high living, a far departure from her first dirt-floored home on the San Pedro, led to talk in Tombstone that Viola had grown haughty and self-impressed. But no one questioned the Slaughters' hospitality.

"It seemed like open house 365 days a year," Wells wrote, "as John and Viola entertained a constant stream of business associates, soldiers, schoolteachers, Arizona rangers, family members, neighbors, surveyors, passersby and friends from all over the Territory."

The Slaughters' time at the San Bernardino ended suddenly and violently. On the night of May 4, 1921, foreman Jesse Fisher was murdered outside the ranch commissary by robbers. Their real target, almost certainly, was John Slaughter. What saved him, Viola swore years later, was the sixth sense he claimed had guided him.

He was ill that night and sitting in his customary spot — by the north window of the main ranch house. Sensing trouble, he asked Fisher to check on the horses. Then John rose and went into the bedroom, out of view. The fatal gunshots came moments later.

The bandits fled, but two of them were captured and convicted. One of them, a 19-year-old Mexican, had spent most of his life working on the ranch. "I felt I'd raised him, but he was one of my boys who did wrong," said Viola.

The time had come to leave the ranch. But Viola had to use her considerable will — and make another speech — to convince her husband. They moved to Douglas in the fall of 1921, and John died early the following year.

Viola lived her remaining years in Douglas, traveling frequently, always eager to correct reporters who sought to portray her famous husband as a grim-faced lawman. But Viola had become something of a frontier character as well. In 1939, she was grand marshal of the town rodeo parade and raced a horse through the streets.

Two years later, Addie came to visit and suffered a heart attack in Viola's home. She died four days later, Febuary 27, 1941. The loss of her adopted daughter, at 68, must have drained Viola's strength. Aunty Slaughter, as she was known to the many children she raised, died a month later. She was 80.

Martha Summerhayes

*She was a soldier's wife thrust into an
uncivilized territory that she described as hostile
to all creatures except snakes and such.
Her description of Indian agents consigns them
to the category of snake: "Of all the unkempt,
unshorn, disagreeable-looking personages
who had ever stepped foot into our quarters,
this was the worst. Heaven save us from a
government which appoints such men as that
to watch over and deal with Indians."*

———⊱⋅⊰———

I F SHE HADN'T BEEN A STODGY, EDUCATED WOMAN FROM SETTLED
New England, and if she hadn't had an eye for anecdote and
a talent for writing, and if her children hadn't badgered
her to sit down 30 years later at her writing desk on Nantucket
Island, amid the chill of a Massachusetts autumn, Arizona
probably would not have known Martha Dunham Summerhayes.

Or perhaps it would be better to say that she would never
have met Arizona. Before the railroad, before ice boxes and
fresh eggs, before settlers could travel without fear of being ambushed and killed — a country she described as "positively
hostile in its attitude towards every living thing except snakes,
centipedes, and spiders."

Martha was born to a well-heeled Nantucket family on
October 21, 1844. At 29, shortly after returning from two years
of studying literature in Germany, she married light-haired,
blue-eyed John Wyer Summerhayes of the U.S. 8th Infantry.
He had hunted whales off the New England coast, trapped

beaver on the Missouri River, and as a Yankee soldier was wounded three times in Civil War battles. With their marriage, Martha said she had "cast her lot with a soldier, and where he was, was home to me."

Life as an army wife took her first to Fort Russell, at Cheyenne, Wyoming, and in the summer of 1874 to Arizona Territory, population about 20,000. To this daughter of privilege, accustomed to the flurry of servants and afternoon lawn tennis, the frontier provided outrages every day.

Imagine her reaction to living in a mud-floored adobe hut and being served by a Cocopah Indian butler clad only in a G-string. Or to staying at a remote ranch owned by Corydon Cooley, a white interpreter and scout with two Indians as wives. "I had to sort over my ideas and deep-rooted prejudices a good many times," she said.

Those words were published in 1908 in *Vanished Arizona*, Martha's account of her four years in the Territory. The book had a modest first printing and was not expected to attract a wide audience. But it took off, is still in print, and some believe it has achieved the status of a classic. While that's arguable, it's certainly a rare view of army life from a woman with colorful opinions and the ability to express them.

On the language of teamsters as they took their wagons over steep places: "Each mule got its share of dreadful curses. I had never heard or conceived of any oaths like those. They made my blood fairly curdle."

On Indian agents: "Of all the unkempt, unshorn, disagreeable-looking personages who had ever stepped foot into our quarters, this was the worst. Heaven save us from a government which appoints such men as that to watch over and deal with Indians."

On life on the Colorado River, where summer temperatures reached 122°F.: "In the late afternoon of each day, a hot steam would collect over the face of the river, then slowly rise, and floating over the length and breadth of this wretched hamlet of Ehrenberg, descend upon and envelope us. Thus we wilted

THIS STYLISH PORTRAIT OF MARTHA SUMMERHAYES
APPEARS IN HER MEMOIRS, WHICH ARE
STILL IN PUBLICATION.

and perspired . . . In a half hour it was gone, but always left me prostrate."

Martha's complaining made fine entertainment, and much of it was about the dust and heat. On their arrival in Arizona in August, 1874, she and Jack traveled about 200 miles by steamship up the Colorado River, from Fort Yuma to Fort Mohave, under a sun so intense "even the wooden arms of the chairs felt as if they were slowly igniting."

The regiment loaded its gear onto prairie-schooner wagons and headed east to Prescott and Fort Whipple. On Martha's first night under army canvas, she slept on a mattress surrounded by a hair lariat to keep rattlesnakes away. Days of hard travel convinced her the desert was a place of horror, especially after witnessing the "suicide" of an officer's dog.

Martha wrote: "Having exhausted his ability to endure, this beautiful red setter fixed his eye upon a distant range of mountains, and ran without turning or heeding any call, straight as the crow flies, towards them and death." A rancher said that he'd seen several dogs do the same thing.

The regiment stayed for three days at Whipple before marching east to Camp Verde. Martha was met there by Mrs. George Brayton, a captain's wife, to whom she complained about Jack's wish that she not carry heavy tinware to their destination at Camp Apache.

"Men think they know everything," Mrs. Brayton said, "but the truth is, they don't know anything. . . . Take all you need, and it will get carried along, somehow."

Martha was learning the way of survival in an army that made more accommodations for camp followers (prostitutes) than it did for officers' wives. The trek to Camp Apache required nearly two months of travel on crude trails over the Mogollon Rim and across terrain controlled by "roving bands of the most cruel tribe ever known, who tortured before they killed."

But the group — about 100 men, five or six officers, two wives, and two laundresses — made it safely, arriving in the fall. Martha was impressed by the picturesque row of log cabins, enormous stables, government buildings, and the sutler's store. Yet, she felt despair after emptying her trunks in the tiny room to which she and Jack had been assigned.

"Oh, Jack! I've nowhere to put things!" she said.

"What things?" he replied.

"Why, all our things," she said, losing her temper.

"Put them back in the chests," he said, "and get them out as you need them." Martha worshipped Jack, always referring to him as "my hero." But love was not optional under circumstances so trying and so foreign.

She got her first, close look at Apaches at the Indians' twice-a-week visits to the camp to receive rations and be counted.

The officers' wives always made time to enjoy the spectacle — the young squaws with their short skirts made of stripped bark, blankets tossed over their shoulders in winter. Men and women wore buckskin garments and, if in high standing in the tribe, necklaces of elk teeth.

Martha saw an older squaw with a horribly disfigured face and learned later that her nose had been cut off for committing adultery.

But the ogling was mutual. On one occasion, Maj. William Worth hosted a dance at his quarters and invited chiefs of the Apache tribe. They arrived, with their squaws, wearing only necklaces and loincloths. Martha noted the "great good looks" of Chief Diablo, who was so charmed by the handsome wife of one of the officers that he asked the husband how many ponies he'd take for her.

Inviting the chiefs to the dance was major breech of convention that caused quite a ripple at camp. "To meet the savage Apache on a basis of social equality," Martha wrote, "and to dance in a quadrille with him! Well, the limit of all things had been reached!"

Another time, boredom sent Martha to a ravine to attend an Apache dance. She wrote of an "unearthly scene" consisting of painted braves, wearing bunches of feathers that gave them the appearance of flying creatures, jumping and shouting around blazing fires. Martha feared for her life when their shouts became warwhoops:

"The demons brandished their knives madly, and nodded their branching horns; the tom-toms were beaten with a dreadful din, and terror seized my heart. What if they be treacherous, and had lured our small party down into the ravine for an ambush! . . . I barely had the strength to climb up the steep side of the hollow . . . to escape."

But savagery ran both ways. Once when Martha heard firing outside the post, Jack grabbed a box for her to stand on to see over the wall. As he did, she heard a thud and smelled something awful, but in the darkness she couldn't see what it was. A soldier told her it was Edam cheese. Later she learned it was a box containing the severed head of an Indian that the camp doctor was saving to take to Washington. Martha was not only seeing the rugged side of life, but experiencing it first-hand. In January, 1875, she gave birth at Camp Apache to a son, Harry. She had to fight to keep him, and herself, alive without fresh vegetables or milk, no woman to serve as nurse, no water for bathing, and an army doctor "much better versed in the sawing off of soldiers' legs than in the treatment of young mothers and babies."

The most trying time came after Jack's transfer to Camp McDowell, outside Phoenix. He and Martha left Camp Apache the second week of April, 1875, along with six troopers and a Mexican guide. She described herself as a "young mother, pale and thin, a child of scarce three months in her arms, and a pistol belt around the waist."

Just short of a defile called Sanford's Pass, the party encountered two hysterical Mexicans who said Apaches had fired upon them, stealing their ponies. The men implored the soldiers, "by the Holy Virgin," not to proceed into the pass. But the men decided to continue, with guns poised. As they started, Jack approached Martha, sitting in a wagon with a cocked derringer in one hand and Harry in the other.

"If I'm hit you'll know what to do," he said. "Don't let them get the baby, for they will carry you both off and, well, the squaws are much more cruel than the bucks. Don't let them get either of you alive." They made it and popped a bottle of champagne to celebrate.

Martha's inability to properly care for Harry forced her back to Nantucket in 1875 for a summer of recuperation. But she missed the blue uniforms, bugle calls, even the monotony, and returned with Jack for more adventures in Arizona, including the discovery of two naked squaws hiding in her kitchen closet at Ehrenberg. One of them was the sister of her Cocopah butler, Charley, who explained, "Bad man go to kill 'em. I hide 'em."

In 1878, Martha and Jack departed Arizona for California.

Later, he was posted at other locations around the country, including another stop in Arizona, in 1886, at the end of the Chief Geronimo campaign. The homecoming was bittersweet. The couple traveled to Tucson on a Pullman car and found an unfamiliar town. Before heading out to Fort Lowell, she and Jack took breakfast at the railroad restaurant.

"Iced cantaloupe was served by a spic-span alert waiter; then quail on toast," she wrote later in her book. "Ice in Arizona? It was like a dream, and I remarked to Jack, 'This isn't the same Arizona we knew in '74,' and then, 'I don't believe I like it as well, either.' "

After Major Summerhayes retired in 1900, he and Martha lived at New Rochelle, New York, in Washington, and on Nantucket Island. Jack died in 1911, two years after *Vanished Arizona* was published. The book was especially popular with military men and students of the West, many of whom wrote admiring letters to Martha.

Among them was Owen Wister, author of *The Virginian*, who mined her experiences as research for a planned story about a frontier woman. Another was Western artist Frederic Remington. He listened to the Summerhayes' experiences, hoping to find grist for paintings. In his letter to Martha, Remington noted how colorful the old army had been and remarked, "Now suppose you had married a man who kept a drug store, see what you would have missed?"

A better question, after so many decades, is what would students of Arizona history have missed? Martha Summerhayes died May 12, 1926, in Schenectady, New York, and is buried beside her "hero" at Arlington National Cemetery.

PHOTOGRAPH CREDITS:

ABOUT THE AUTHOR
PAGE 4   Leo W. Banks. Edward McCain.

ABOUT THE ARTIST
PAGE 5   Veryl Goodnight, courtesy of the artist.

INTRODUCTION
PAGE 9   Elizabeth Heiser. Arizona Historical Society/Flagstaff.
PAGE 11   King Woolsey home. Arizona Historical Society/Tucson, #6624.
PAGE 15   Elizabeth Aughey Young. Fort Verde State Historic Park.
PAGE 18   Mollie Fly. Arizona Historical Society/Tucson, AHS#9891.
PAGE 19   Sarah Herring Sorin. Arizona Historical Society/Tucson,
          AHS#17431.
PAGE 22   Cordelia Kay. Mohave County Historical Society, #6421.
PAGE 24   Nampeyo. Arizona Department of Library, Archives and
          Public Records, Archives Division, Phoenix.

CHAPTER ONE
PAGE 28   Mary Bernard Aguirre. Arizona Historical Society/Tucson,
          AHS#51.

CHAPTER TWO
PAGE 35   Sarah Bowman's gravestone. Arizona Historical Society/Tucson,
          AHS#63795.
PAGE 38   Lithograph of Fort Yuma. Arizona Pioneers' Historical Society
          Library.

CHAPTER THREE
PAGE 43   Nellie Cashman. Arizona Historical Society/Tucson, #1847.
PAGE 46   Nellie Cashman in hat. Arizona Historical Society/Tucson, #83.

CHAPTER FOUR
PAGE 51   Pauline Cushman in uniform. Arizona Historical Society/Tucson,
          #234.
PAGE 54   Pauline Cushman. The National Portrait Galley, Smithsonian
          Institution, NPG.80.219.

CHAPTER FIVE
PAGE 58   Josephine and Wyatt Earp. Arizona Historical Society/Tucson,
          AHS#76627.

CHAPTER SIX
PAGE 66   Ida Genung. Prescott Sharlot Hall Museum, PO-2350.2P.

CHAPTER SEVEN
PAGE 72   Pearl Hart in prison stripes. Arizona Historical Society/Tucson,
          AHS#9183.
PAGE 74   Pearl Hart with rifle. Arizona Historical Society/Tucson,
          AHS#28916.
PAGE 77   Pearl Hart in Yuma Territorial Prison. Yuma Territorial Prison
          State Historic Park Archives.

CHAPTER EIGHT
PAGE 83   Josephine Brawley Hughes. Arizona Department of Library,
          Archives and Public Records, Archives Division, Phoenix, #97-6546.

CHAPTER NINE
PAGE 89   Emma Lee French. Arizona Historical Society/Flagstaff, #666-275.
PAGE 90   John D. Lee. Arizona Historical Society/Tucson, #12001.

**PAULINE CUSHMAN (LEFT)
AND NELLIE CASHMAN**
Both were women of unusual
accomplishment, yet Pauline Cushman
and Nellie Cashman could not have
been more different. Pauline lived
for the applause, yet died in a
downward spiral of self-destruction.
Nellie pursued her own adventures
with as much enthusiasm as her many
charities, a character who lived life
with gusto into her 70s.

DAYS OF DESTINY
Fate Beckons Desperados & Lawmen

Many a newcomer journeyed West intent on molding his own future — grabbing life with both hands and producing opportunity. Shifty or bold, desperate or noble, given a trusty horse, a gun, and occasional friends, any man might stand a chance.

But every chain of events has one single day, perhaps a fleeting moment, when fate first points a decisive finger and the course of history changes. Delve into this collection of 20 Wild West tales and see how real-life desperados and lawmen faced momentous days that changed their lives forever.

Does the outlaw finally dance to his doom? Will the lynch mob hang the gambler who just killed a man? Does the kidnapped boy stay with the Apaches who stole him? Will the young mother become a stagecoach robber? Look back through time to see if you can spot when destiny dealt the final hand.

Softcover. 144 pages. **#ADAP6 $7.95**

MANHUNTS & MASSACRES

Cleverly staged ambushes, horrific massacres, and dogged pursuits catapult the reader into days of savagery on the Arizona frontier. If life was hard, death came even harder: A bungled robbery leads to murder. Arizona's largest manhunt unjustly imprisons two brothers. Sleeping cowboys are ambushed in Guadalupe Canyon. Bloodstained cash traps a family's desperate killer.

Reading through these 18 accounts, you'll join the posses in hot pursuit across the roughest terrain and outwit the most suspicious of fugitive outlaws. From the vicious to the valiant, each true story will convince you — the good old days were a challenge that few of us could survive!

Softcover. 144 pages. **#AMMP7 $7.95**

To order these books or to request a catalog, contact:
Arizona Highways, 2039 West Lewis Avenue, Phoenix, AZ 85009-2893.
Or send a fax to 602-254-4505. Or call toll-free nationwide 1-800-543-5432.
(In the Phoenix area or outside the U.S., call 602-258-1000.)
Visit us at http://www.arizonahighways.com to order online.

THEY LEFT THEIR MARK
Heroes and Rogues of Arizona History

Indians, scouts, ranchers, and mountain men are vividly remembered here in 16 true stories of Western adventure. Before Arizona Territory was ever surveyed, mapped, or named, its serrated mountains, savage deserts, and extreme temperatures demanded much of those first peoples who already knew it and those newcomers who were driven to explore it.

Generations passed into memory. Yet even as more settlers and opportunists came to the Southwest, the land resisted their efforts to tame it, remaining fiercely rugged from horizon to horizon.

Those whose names are recalled in these accounts were individualists who left their unique stamp — whether good or bad — forever on Arizona's history:

Alchesay, the Apache who faced monumental changes to successfully lead his people in war and in peace;

Dr. Goodfellow, the Tombstone surgeon whose bloody field experiences made him a national expert on bullet wounds;

James Addison Reavis, the swindler who almost became a Spanish baron with his own Arizona kingdom; and many more. Through their lives, experience those early days of struggle and discovery.

Softcover. 144 pages. Black and white historical photographs.
#ATMP7 $7.95

VOLUME 4
WILD WEST
COLLECTION

THE LAW OF THE GUN

Recounting the colorful lives and careers of gunfighters, lawmen, and outlaws, historian and author Marshall Trimble examines the mystique of the Old West and the role that guns have played in that fascination.

Tools of survival as well as deadly weapons, guns on the American frontier came to symbolize the guts and independence that people idealized in their Western heroes — even when those "heroes" were cold-blooded killers.

With the deft touch of a master storyteller, Trimble recounts the macabre humor of digging up one dead gunslinger to deliver his last shot of whiskey, the intensity of the Arizona Rangers who faced death down a gun barrel every time they pursued a crook, and the vengeful aftermath of Wyatt Earp's showdown in Tombstone. Each gripping tale will make you want to read more of how guns determined life in the West.

Softcover. 192 pages. Black and white historical photographs.
#AGNP7 $8.95

ARIZONA
HIGHWAYS
BOOKS

To order these books or to request a catalog, contact:
Arizona Highways, 2039 West Lewis Avenue, Phoenix, AZ 85009-2893.
Or send a fax to 602-254-4505. Or call toll-free nationwide 1-800-543-5432.
(In the Phoenix area or outside the U.S., call 602-258-1000.)
Visit us at http://www.arizonahighways.com to order online.

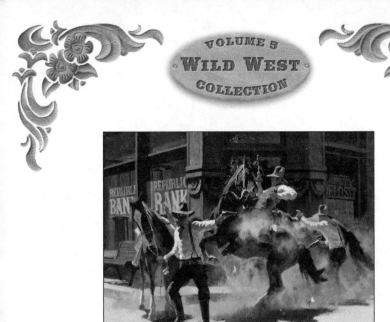

TOMBSTONE CHRONICLES
Tough Folks, Wild Times

Ed Schieffelin's hunger for the thrill of discovery survived brutal terrain and warring Apaches. When he at last struck silver in the middle of nowhere, thousands flocked to a rough mining camp that would become . . . Tombstone.

Rubbing shoulders with Clanton, Earp, and Holliday, ordinary people lived real life in extraordinary times as Tombstone became an oasis of decadence, cosmopolitan culture, and reckless violence.

Johnny Ringo was "King of the Cowboys," until he turned up dead quite mysteriously. Curly Bill Brocius, a bully with a sense of rhythm, set folks dancing . . . at gunpoint. Reverend Peabody landed some punches for the gospel. Theirs are some of 17 true stories from an Old West where anything could happen — and too often did.

Softcover. 144 pages. Black and white historical photographs.
#AWTP8 $7.95

To order these books or to request a catalog, contact:
Arizona Highways, 2039 West Lewis Avenue, Phoenix, AZ 85009-2893.
Or send a fax to 602-254-4505. Or call toll-free nationwide 1-800-543-5432.
(In the Phoenix area or outside the U.S., call 602-258-1000.)
Visit us at http://www.arizonahighways.com to order online.

VOLUME 7
WILD WEST
COLLECTION

INTO THE UNKNOWN
Adventure on the Spanish Colonial Frontier

Centuries before Wyatt Earp and Billy the Kid rode onto the scene, Spanish-speaking pioneers and gunslingers roamed regions including what now is the American West. They didn't pretend to be saints. They gambled and swore, shot up their friends, and had tempestuous affairs. Going where no non-Indian had gone before, they lived and died in a wild new world, lured — even driven — by the power and appeal of the unknown.

It was a time of unmatchable heroism and unimaginable tragedy, set in uncharted territory that would someday become Kansas, Oklahoma, Texas, Nebraska, New Mexico, Arizona, California, Oregon, Washington, Utah, British Columbia, Colorado, Alaska.

A castaway-turned-slave becomes the West's first loner, first fugitive, and first tragic hero — all before 1540. An English pirate tries to steal California. A German lands in the Inquisition's snares. Outlaws die in a ring of fire. A sailor walks from the Pacific Northwest to Chihuahua. Unbelievable, even outrageous, but all true, these tales of courage, mayhem, and disaster by award-winning history writer Susan Hazen-Hammond take lovers of the Wild West into a vast unknown and put them in touch with a passionate, powerful past that has been neglected too long.

Softcover. 144 pages. Illustrated. #ASCS9 $7.95

Coming in October 1999

No Turning Back
by Veryl Goodnight

Too young and naive
to think they could fail
Too full of visions
for the end of the trail
They stored their silk dresses
and donned calico
To join in the cry
of Westward Ho

Their diaries tell
of the endless hours
The vast sea of grass
and bounty of wildflowers
They tell of children
conceived and born
And of those who were buried
in the gray silent morn

Still the wagons rolled on
and the ruts got deeper
The column moved westward
as the route got steeper
Teams dropped from exhaustion
in the summer heat
As the emigrants pressed on
defying defeat

They met Indians who were friends
and many that were foe
They saw days of drought
and blinding snow
Only one thing was certain
along this wagon track
There was absolutely —
No Turning Back